Apple Muffin *cottage*

Vicki Eileen McGuire

Trilogy Christian Publishers

A Wholly Owned Subsidiary of Trinity Broadcasting Network

2442 Michelle Drive

Tustin, CA 92780

Copyright © 2024 by Vicki Eileen McGuire

Scripture quotations marked AMP are taken from the Amplified® Bible (AMP), Copyright © 2015 by The Lockman Foundation. Used by permission. www.Lockman.org. Scripture quotations marked NKJV are taken from the New King James Version®. Copyright © 1982 by Thomas Nelson. Used by permission. All rights reserved. Scripture quotations marked KJV are taken from the King James Version of the Bible. Public domain.

All rights reserved, including the right to reproduce this book or portions thereof in any form whatsoever.

For information, address Trilogy Christian Publishing

Rights Department, 2442 Michelle Drive, Tustin, Ca 92780.

Trilogy Christian Publishing/ TBN and colophon are trademarks of Trinity Broadcasting Network.

For information about special discounts for bulk purchases, please contact Trilogy Christian Publishing.

Trilogy Disclaimer: The views and content expressed in this book are those of the author and may not necessarily reflect the views and doctrine of Trilogy Christian Publishing or the Trinity Broadcasting Network.

10 9 8 7 6 5 4 3 2 1

Library of Congress Cataloging-in-Publication Data is available.

ISBN: 979-8-89041-410-6

E-ISBN: 979-8-89041-411-3

"I am the vine, you are the branches. He who abides in Me, and I in him, bears much fruit… By this My Father is glorified, that you bear much fruit; so you will be My disciples."

John 15:5, 8 (NKJV)

To all of my loved ones who lived this endeavor with me, who gave me names, ideas, direction, and encouragement throughout its creation and listened endlessly to each written word, checked my credibility, and believed that one day I would actually complete this task—thank you. I love you all, and may you always bear good fruit so you may be His disciples.

Special thanks to Carrie Beth for naming Apple Muffin Cottage.

This is a work of fiction. Names, characters, places and incidents either are the product of the author's imagination or are used fictitiously and any resemblance to actual persons, living or dead, business establishments, events or locales is entirely coincidental.

Table of Contents

Chapter 1: Grammy's Exit 11

Chapter 2: Apple Muffin Cottage 23

Chapter 3: Thomas Henry's Funeral 29

Chapter 4: A Refuge from the Cold 43

Chapter 5: Secrets and Treasures In the Attic 53

Chapter 6: The Mice Upstairs 69

Chapter 7: Gracie Ponders the Harvest 73

Chapter 8: Gracie's Memories 83

Chapter 9: Miss Patsy Stops by with the
"Seacrick" Ingredient 97

Chapter 10: Thanksgiving at Apple Muffin Cottage. . .109

Chapter 11: Grammy's Gift 129

Chapter 12: Going with J.T. 143

Chapter 13: Trees 157

Chapter 14: A Night for Miracles 179

Chapter 15: Trying to Move Forward 199

Chapter 16: Humdrum Days 207

Chapter 17: Meadows' Grocery 1969 211

Chapter 18: Meadows' Grocery—Your Friendly
    Neighborhood Store—2002 217

Chapter 19: Hope Springs Eternal 225

Chapter 20: Working for Ian.....................231

Chapter 21: Viney's Condition 241

Chapter 22: Dinky Makes His Own Fun
    When Miss Patsy Comes for Tea 247

Chapter 23: Blasts from the Past.................263

Chapter 24: Promises Kept......................281

Grammy's and Gracie's Favorite Recipes and Crafts. .309

Chapter 1:

Grammy's Exit

March 1, 1998

The six chimes of the mantel clock in the living room were muffled by the chaotic sounds of weather outside. The morning was dark, wet, and wild. February left quietly at midnight, but March was ushered in with lion-like winds that shook the old walls of the farmhouse, known in recent years to all of Farmwell Valley as Apple Muffin Cottage. Fierce rain pummeled the antique panes of glass in Grammy's room, where she lay dying.

This ground on which the house sat had been in the Barton family since Isaiah Barton surveyed a large tract of land in the western wilderness of Virginia, which is now the state of West Virginia, near the Ohio River, for General George Washington in 1771. He was paid in a large portion of that land, which became known as Farmwell Valley, along with, it was speculated, some silver.

Many years later, his great-grandson, Jacob Barton,

lived on inherited wealth from the selling off of land through the generations, leaving only one hundred and twenty acres to the Barton family. He did nothing much all day but play his fiddle, chew tobacco, and drink rum, but it was he who had the house built in 1855 for his wife and ten children. Later generations added on until the original structure was doubled in size.

He was an eccentric rapscallion who, being drunk and fearful of the "rebels" as they purportedly were to come through his valley during the Civil War, hid his family's fortune but couldn't remember just where. Although he'd written down clues in the family Bible that day as to its location, nobody seemed to know what they meant, and neither did he once he sobered up—much to his dismay.

So, from then on, necessity of survival dictated he work his land. He and his five sons cleared it, planted the first trees in the orchards (subsequent generations planted more), and all the family helped to farm the rest. Over time, Spirit Creek Farm and Orchards became so successful, it was the envy of all who lived in Farmwell Valley.

Legend has it, he eventually saw the loss of his fortune as divine intervention that did him and his family good, and he became a very devout man. From time to time, he was heard praying fervently in his woods, playing hymns on his fiddle, and asking the good Lord to reveal the whereabouts of his fortune.

In 1945, Thomas Henry Barton inherited the farm from his late father, Charles. Later that year, he married Grace Victoria Gibson, and it had been her home ever since. Today, their bedroom overlooked the winter-dormant apple orchards full of hardy apple trees—wine sap, grime's golden and its offspring—the golden delicious. They grew other fruit, as well. Cherries, peaches, plums, and pears grew abundantly along Spirit Creek. For years now, it was also the place where Barton family roots grew deep in good soil.

"The apples are ready to be picked, Thomas! We'll have to hurry now," Grace cried out.

The room was cool, damp, and drafty as rain continued drumming a sad cadence against the glass.

"It's okay, Grammy," her younger grandson J.T. quieted her, eased her back onto her pillow, and tucked a quilt around her frail shoulders.

His grandfather Thomas, or Pop, as he was known to his grandchildren, died last year in an orchard at sunset on a cool fall evening. He'd been out picking some of the last of the wine saps, but Grace found him face down on the ground with an empty basket by his side, the apples spilled around him.

"As long as we've been married, he's always come in for supper. That's why I went lookin' for him. I knew somethin' was wrong," she told her grandchildren the night he passed away, between quiet sobs.

"Even after your daddy passed away in Vietnam, Pop would come in and just sit with us at the table, wouldn't eat a bite. Just sat but always came in."

Grace and Thomas weathered the storm of Joshua's passing because *his* four young children needed them. They couldn't afford the luxury of getting lost in their sorrow. The grandchildren's Irish mother, Maggie, was so bereft after their father died that she left and never returned. Some people in the valley said she'd done away with herself. Others said she'd just lost her mind from grief and ran off. There'd been speculation that maybe she went back home to Ireland. Some unkind people gossiped and said she'd run off to Woodstock in August of '69 with a long-haired hippie. *But who really knew where she was?*

Years later, their older granddaughter Gracie's husband Ben was killed, and she was left with two little ones to raise alone, so Grammy and Pop were there for them, too.

Grammy's Exit

The Bartons' lot in life had been love and loss, joy and sorrow, but always together.

Grammy's life was waning now. It was being emptied out like the apple basket she'd picked up from the ground beside Thomas the day he died. His death was her queue to leave. Grace Victoria Gibson Barton was eternally secure and ready to meet her maker. She had accepted Christ as her savior one night at bedtime when she was just nine years old. Her mother explained to her that Jesus was the Son of God who had been crucified and died on an old wooden cross to take away our sins, but on the third day, He rose up again. He was victorious over death, hell, and the grave so that all who believe in Him would receive the free gift of salvation and live forever in heaven. That night, her mother taught her a scripture from the Bible:

> *"For God so loved the world, that he gave his only begotten Son, that whosoever believeth in Him should not perish, but have everlasting life."*
>
> **John 3:16 (KJV)**

So, she asked Jesus to cleanse her from sin, live in her heart forever, and help her be faithful to Him always. A month later, she was baptized in Spirit Creek with all of Hope Springs Church watching. It was a decision she'd never regretted.

All of her grandchildren had been saved and baptized except for J.T., but she trusted he would, eventually, come to accept the Lord. She'd trained him up in the way that he should go. She'd put him in Jesus' hands. So, inevitably, someday…

Grammy longed to go to heaven. Her race had been run, and she knew the good Lord hadn't meant for her to live very long without her Thomas. So, after he passed and while she still had a little strength left, she enlisted J.T.'s help to start packing up the pieces of her life.

"No one ever had to clean up after me since I was old enough to clean up after myself," she stated proudly, "and no one ever will."

So, for days and weeks, they cleared out drawers, cabinets, closets, attic, garage, and barn, neatly packing up the remnants of her life into plastic tubs and cardboard boxes, labeling each with permanent marker as they went. Some things were only "fit for the garbage" or to be burned. When their herculean task was complete, J.T. put her many containers in the attic, at Grammy's request, along with all the other family relics and Christmas decorations, where they could be found and done with as her family pleased.

Grammy's Exit

There were boxes of craft supplies, photos and photo albums, fabric, patterns, and thread from her sewing and quilting, seeds from the orchard, seeds from her flower and vegetable gardens, tried and true recipes and cookbooks from her bakery and kitchen, favorite record albums, eight-tracks, cassettes and CDs, every greeting card and letter from loved ones and some boxes held *secret* things that, after she was gone, could be revealed.

There was a special box that held her old family Bibles, except for the one her mother had given her on her thirteenth birthday (she intended to be buried with that one), and daily devotionals she loved and collected through the years. She'd kept some Sunday school literature that she'd taught the young children out of at Hope Springs Church.

There were also boxes for each of her grandchildren and great-grandchildren that were filled with every long-dried leaf picked up by their tiny hands, baby shoes, outfits, blankets, rattles, and engraved silver spoons. Every drawing made for her and kept on the refrigerator had been stored along with their Sunday school papers, Vacation Bible School crafts, Certificates of Baptisms, report cards, and scrapbooks. There was even a box of Joshua's things that she could never bear to part with.

Once everything was in the attic, she then began to put her affairs in order. All of her bills were paid, final letters were written to family and friends, and her Last Will and Testament was legally revised, signed, and notarized. Everything was finished.

She could rest peacefully now. Her time had come. Her race was run. Her life was ebbing out from her body now, like water being poured from a bucket. So, she took to her sickbed in her room in her beloved Apple Muffin Cottage.

As she waited, she found much comfort in the scriptures and from the presence of her family.

"If the same Spirit that raised Jesus from the dead lives in you, and He does, He will raise you up, Grammy," her older grandson Michael, the pastor, told her reassuringly.

Yes, He does, and it is well with my soul.

"In my house are many mansions," he continued reading from the Book of Matthew. "If it were not so, I would have told you."

I know He has prepared a place for me, and I'm longing to see it. I'll be waiting for you all.

Softly, her granddaughters, Gracie and LaVinia, wept and sang an old hymn their grandmother and grandfather sung often:

Grammy's Exit

Shall we gather at the river,

Where bright angel feet have trod;

With its crystal tide forever

Flowing by the throne of God?

Yes, we'll gather at the river,

The beautiful, the beautiful river;

Gather with the saints at the river

That flows by the throne of God.

With an angelic smile on her face and a youthful gleam in her eye, she pointed to the empty rocking chair that sat in a darkened corner of the room and said convincingly, "Pop's here! Do ya see him? And look, Gracie, there's Ben!"

For an hour or more, she talked to her departed loved ones in tender, hushed tones. "Mom, is that you? I've missed you," she said and smiled faintly.

Finally, reaching for J.T.'s hand, she whispered weakly to him, "I'll be watchin' for you. And I'll see you again. All who call on the name of the Lord shall be saved."

"I know, Grammy," he said to her while tears streamed down his handsome face. He kissed her limp hand tenderly. "Oh, Grammy," J.T. whispered, "I'm gonna miss you."

"You know where I'll be." She smiled at him and turned and looked at Gracie.

"I trust you to take care of the fruit—all of it. You're the best one to do it. I trust ya!"

"Yes, Grammy, I sure will." Gracie, knowing her grandmother meant not only the fruit in the orchards but the souls of all her family, brushed her grandmother's hair away from her face, kissed her cheek, and told her she loved her.

"I love you, too—very much." Grammy's voice could hardly be heard now.

"Grammy!" LaVinia cried. "We've come a long way together…"

"And we still have a long way to go," Grammy whispered, finishing the saying that she always said to her grandchildren at bedtime to reassure them she wouldn't leave.

Then, suddenly, Grammy Grace Barton looked upward. As her eyes sparkled with excitement, she said ever so sweetly with a very grateful heart, "Thank You, Jesus, for coming to get me."

Then, she closed her eyes peacefully and gracefully entered her rest.

Chapter 2:

Apple Muffin Cottage

"...and weep with them that weep."

Romans 12:15 (KJV)

November 2001

Thomas Henry, the old one-eyed black cat, had died of natural causes. Gracie Barton LeMaster peeked through the living room window of Apple Muffin Cottage to see the little band of mourners standing in the front yard, waiting in the bitter cold for the arrival of his makeshift hearse. She wiped away a tear with one hand and held back the faded blue and white gingham curtains with the other.

"Bless their hearts," she said as she pitied her two children and their cousins for having to bury Thomas Henry in this cold and because there'd been too many funerals in the last few years. She wondered how they'd all survived such loss.

In spite of her sadness, though, the familiarity of the now-flimsy curtains brought a slight smile to her lips as she remembered how every spring, for almost twenty years, Grammy had starched and ironed them stiff.

"I hate droopy curtains," her lively grandmother would say resolutely while standing by her ironing board, wielding her Sunbeam steam iron in and out between each pleat with great care and precision. Once re-hung, the homemade curtains looked as good as new and better than store-bought, Grammy would always announce.

The sweet hominess of her grandparent's living room had often comforted her, especially on her hardest days when she'd waited for her mother to return, but she never did. Its calm serenity, glowing coals in the fireplace, Grammy's sewing basket beside her rocker, her Bible on a small table nearby, and the scent of freshly baked apple muffins wafting from the kitchen—all gave her a confident assurance down through the years of a constant refuge.

The day she learned Ben had been killed in Honduras, she ran home to Grammy and Pop. When Pop died, she came home for Grammy, and when Grammy took to her sickbed, she took a leave of absence from work to be with her until she passed—but now, she was home to stay and to heal.

Apple Muffin Cottage, with its welcoming red front door, white lap siding, and black shutters, along with thirty acres and the fruit orchards, now belonged to Gracie. Grammy left them to her, along with instructions to take good care of the *fruit*. Not in her own power, but with the help of God, she would do her level best to take care of what Grammy had entrusted to her.

The rest of Spirit Creek Farm had been parceled out to LaVinia and J.T. a few years ago, and Michael's portion had been sold to put him through seminary and to give him a start in life.

Running parallel to the orchards was Spirit Creek, which crisscrossed through the whole farm and continued on right through the heart of Farmwell Valley.

"Looks like it could snow," Gracie whispered to herself as she considered the dark, heavy clouds through the chilled glass, now getting foggy from her breath. She dropped the curtains, wiped the dust off her hands onto her apron, and made a mental note to buy some new ones. *It was time.*

Then she grabbed the poker, stoked the fire until ashes

and small glowing embers fell through the grate onto the inside of the hearth, and added another log to the burning heap. The old floor furnace was good at heating the center of the house, but the outer rooms and upstairs got very cold.

"At least they'll have a good fire and a nice warm supper when they come in," she again whispered to herself as she shuffled back to the kitchen in her house slippers.

The stark white kitchen in Apple Muffin Cottage was well-packed but efficient. Coming in from the dining room, you could see an electric stove just inside the kitchen door to the left beside the refrigerator. On the right of the entrance was an antique red and white Hoosier cabinet, which was brought in by horse and wagon during the teens by Thomas' dad—a Christmas present for his wife, Nancy Jane. Across from both, at the very back of the room, was an antique Majestic cast iron wood-burning stove made in the 1890s that Grammy would never give up because it was *perfect for canning*. It was black and hulk-like, still in use, but primarily for heating the backside of the old farmhouse. J.T. kept kindling in an old apple crate stamped *Spirit Creek Farm and Orchards* in the corner and stove wood on the back porch.

A small round table sat in the middle of the room.

Sitting at it provided a view (through red and white curtains that framed the old window above the sink) of meadows and barn. In all of Apple Muffin Cottage, this had been Grammy's favorite place, and now, it was Gracie's.

The antique furnishings reflected the bygone days at Apple Muffin Cottage, but Gracie's laptop computer spoke of a new era of information and future possibilities. She'd made a place for it on the table where there was easy access to both phone and electric outlets. Grammy's "bakery" extension, where she'd taken orders for her baked goods, hadn't been used for years. Now, it had a new purpose as a dial-up line for logging in and connecting to the world wide web.

Gracie found Grammy's potato masher in a drawer. She poured melted butter and scalded milk, along with salt and pepper, onto drained potatoes and mashed them in the big white bowl just like Grammy had done thousands of times before, and as she worked, her mind wandered back to thoughts of Thomas Henry. *What a shame about that ole cat!*

He never really bothered anybody. However, it wasn't unusual for a kind neighbor or two to find him every now and then on their property hunting ground squirrels, fishing in a cool stream, or just sitting on a rock enjoying a shady glen dappled with sunlight. Most never considered him an interloper, though, but a welcome friend.

He was a terrific mouser with a bit of a wanderlust, but he never failed to come home. Even when a fight with another cat or an angry raccoon damaged his left eye so severely that a vet in Brotherton had to remove it, he still made his way back to Spirit Creek Farm, although half blind. So, it was only fitting he have a nice funeral and be buried under the big oak tree on the hill above the cellar house overlooking his home, the old, weathered gray barn where he chased mice and rats.

Earlier in the day, Gracie's younger brother J.T., with a heavy heart, went to the garage to make a small casket for Thomas Henry. On his way back, he noticed that the smoke spouting from the old rock chimney of Apple Muffin Cottage rose only so high before it swirled downward close to the ground. This was a sure sign, according to old-timers, that snow was on the way. If it *was* a true indication, he guessed Farmwell Valley would soon have its first snowfall of the season.

Chapter 3:

Thomas Henry's Funeral

Blessed are those who mourn; for they shall be comforted.

Matthew 5:4 (NKJV)

There was a threatening steel-gray November sky above the mourner's heads, punctuated now and then by silhouettes of Canadian geese on the wing, honking loudly as they flew over in a "v" formation. For now, though, there was not a snowflake in sight as the small group waited and shivered in the bitter cold.

"I'm freezin', Elizabeth," said a very little boy with his head tilted back, looking from underneath a black silk top hat that was much too big for his head. He also wore an oversized hounds-tooth sport coat, from the 1960s, with sleeves twice as long as his arms.

"I know, Dink! We all are," his big sister answered him just as an almost deliberate frigid gust of wind blew her curly auburn hair, the color of apple butter, away from her rosy cheeks, revealing her beautiful face. It also swept the purple plume on top of her vintage hat backward. The young girl had delicate pixie-like features, small ears that stuck out from her head slightly, a cute upturned nose, and green almond-shaped eyes.

Callie Ann's eyes were brighter green, but she was a big calico cat who, at present, was draped over the girl's shoulder. She'd been Elizabeth's plaything for years. Having suffered many indignities for this cause, she was now resigned to her circumstances and totally indifferent to the old yellowed baby bonnet on her head tied in a bow under her chin.

Elizabeth thought herself to be the perfect summation of style and beauty today. She was pleased to have found Great-Great-Grandma Nancy Jane Barton's hat in the attic trunk and Great-Aunt Belle's really long and warm black coat with the very large mother-of-pearl buttons on a hook under the eaves. It hung clear to the tops of Grammy's gold-buckled, spool-heeled shoes and covered up all traces of her blue jeans and white sport socks.

"Here, Dinky," their cousin Victoria said sweetly, "you can have my scarf. Wrap it around your neck, and it'll help keep your face warm."

Thomas Henry's Funeral

"Fanks, Skippy." Skippy was a nickname her dad had given her.

"But I can't do it. I don't gots no hands." He waved the ends of the empty jacket sleeves in the air as the big black hat fell down over his eyes.

"Yeah, ya do. They're in there somewhere," Victoria giggled. "Here, I'll help you." She wound the royal blue and wine-colored scarf around and around Dinky's neck until she covered up part of his mouth and the bottoms of his ears. "Is that better?"

"Yeah." Dinky's voice was muffled.

"But hold that stupid hat up over your face or carry it," Elizabeth ordered.

"I wonder if ole Thomas Henry's cold. Is he, Elizabeth?"

"I don't think it matters, Dink. He won't know about it if he is," Elizabeth answered quickly. The question made her feel sad because she'd loved Thomas Henry. He had always been part of their lives, and now he was gone, too, just like their dad, Grammy, and Pop.

Victoria started to shake slightly. Her very large sky-blue eyes, now misty with tears underneath lengthy black lashes, were Elizabeth's envy. Her hands were tucked warmly into Grammy's old white rabbit fur muff. Her silky blonde hair, topped by a red velvet bonnet, fell straight onto her tiny shoulders. A gray crocheted shawl covered her own jacket, but she was still cold. She had unselfishly given Dinky the scarf that was keeping her face and neck warm. She was wearing a pair of her mom's old high heels that she wore to a prom in high school. They were big and floppy and let cold air in around her small feet, even though she had on thick socks.

"Here, guys," Elizabeth ordered, "let's huddle closer together to help keep the wind off us." Each one took a step in closer towards the other.

Then, with heartfelt sympathy and the awareness that she looked wonderful, Elizabeth hugged Callie Ann close with gloved hands. Adding a touch of drama, which was usual for Elizabeth, she whispered, "Poor Callie Ann, I'm so sorry about your brother." The silver, cream, and peach-colored cat squeezed her eyes shut a little bit tighter from the wind—still indifferent.

The two of them had gotten to know each other well in the Apple Muffin Cottage kitchen, where Callie Ann had been a mouser, too. Grammy Grace Barton, at one time, was the unofficial baker for Hope Springs. For years, she baked fruit pies, fruit cobblers, and apple muffins for the

Thomas Henry's Funeral

local grocery store bakery and wedding cakes for neighbors occasionally. Whenever Elizabeth visited, she enlisted her help, and they always tried a new recipe or two.

"A natural!" Grammy always declared that her great-granddaughter had a gift. It was Elizabeth's favorite thing in the whole world to do—bake and spend time with Grammy and Callie Ann in the kitchen at Apple Muffin Cottage—and it pleased Grammy to know she was passing on her most treasured recipes to someone who appreciated them.

Sometimes, Thomas Henry was let in to warm up by the old wood stove while they were having tea and enjoying some of Grammy's famous apple muffins.

"Poor Thomas Henry," whispered Elizabeth under her breath as she remembered their good times—now gone forever.

While the mourners continued to wait, the aroma of fried chicken, homemade apple pie, biscuits, wood smoke, and dry leaves mingled with the cold air to make a wonderful autumn smell. They all were hungry, still freezing, and growing very impatient.

"Hurry up, William," Elizabeth shouted. Something had started to irritate her neck. She took one arm from around Callie Ann long enough to scratch.

"I'm coming. Hold your horses," moaned Victoria's brother William, who pulled a good-sized, squeaky red wagon with a small license plate on the back that read *Joshua*. It carried a small wooden box containing Thomas Henry's remains. He stopped in front of where a gate used to be, just on the other side of the old wooden fence.

"What a mess," Elizabeth whispered with disgust. She could barely tolerate her cousin, who was close to her age. He'd always been a thorn in her side. Oversized ears were all that held Pop's dirty, old, wide-brimmed hat just above his eyes. His coat sleeves were too long, too, and his pant legs draped over the tops of Pop's big, clunky brown shoes, now thick with mud.

"Ya'll line up!" William called to the mourners.

"It's about time," grumbled Elizabeth, "we're just about to freeze to death."

"Well, get movin' then. That'll warm ya up."

"Humpff!" His cousin was disgruntled, but still yet she began to sing as, one by one, they all fell in line behind the wagon and joined in singing:

Thomas Henry's Funeral

Shall we gather at the river,

Where bright angel feet have trod;

They passed the remains of a long unused coal pile and turned right at the old garage. As they crossed a trickling brook that fed into Spirit Creek, they continued up the hill along the narrow gravel road to a huge old oak tree up above the cellar house—along the way, passing deep woods littered with old bee boxes and barren trees.

"What's that?" Victoria halted. Slightly frightened, she asked, "Did you hear that?"

"Hear what?" Elizabeth questioned.

"I thought I heard violin music." Victoria tilted her head to one side, curiously listening again for the sound.

"Probably just the wind," offered William.

"Yeah, probably," she agreed with a puzzled look on her face but was not convinced.

"Don't be goofy, Victoria!" Elizabeth chastised her cousin. The procession continued their funeral march accompanied by the squeak of the wagon:

With its crystal tide forever

Flowing by the throne of God?

Yes, we'll gather at the river,

The beautiful, the beautiful river;

Gather with the saints at the river

That flows by the throne of God.

The mournful rhythm ensued until they stopped and circled around the little grave that William had helped his Uncle J.T. dig earlier.

"Look!" Victoria pointed upward. "We'd better hurry."

Suddenly, big white snowflakes were falling rapidly from the sky like goose down being shaken out of a torn bed pillow. William took the small coffin off the wagon hurriedly, put it in the ground, then stood back.

"Well, I'd just like to say," he said with his hat now in his hand, choking back tears, "that old Thomas Henry was about the best friend, even if he was a cat, a person could have. We've had some really good times together, and it was good knowin' him."

"Goodbye, Thomas Henry." Dinky sniffed and waved a loose coat sleeve at the dead cat.

"We'd better hurry up, guys," William directed. Snow

Thomas Henry's Funeral

was accumulating fast on the cold ground.

"Goodbye, Thomas Henry." With tears running down her cheeks, Victoria stepped forward, pulled a wilted yellow mum out of her muff, and threw it into the open grave.

Her mother, LaVinia, had pinched off the last bloom from the pot on their front porch this morning. "For Thomas Henry," she'd said.

"Goodbye, Thomas Henry," Elizabeth said as she sniffed and scratched her neck.

William quickly tossed in shovelfuls of dirt, making sure his friend was properly covered over.

Victoria leaned over, kissed the *resigned* cat on top of the head, and said, "I'm *so* sorry about your brother, Callie Ann."

"Let's get on with it!" Elizabeth snapped, impatient with Victoria's emotional display. "Let's all bow our heads and pray!" The others looked at her with surprise. "Dear Lord," Elizabeth took the lead with an almost operatic flair, seizing her opportunity for more drama. William kept one eye open and looked at her as she continued.

"We thank Thee for the life of our dear, now departed

friend, Thomas Henry. He was so good, so kind, so loved, and so cherished by us all. We place him in Thy loving arms to care for him throughout eternity because… because…" She stammered and halted.

"Dear God!" Elizabeth yelled. "Something's chewing my neck off!" She lost her concentration as she continued to scratch wildly with one gloved hand. "This cat's eaten up with fleas, and they're all over me!"

"Y'all pray for Elizabeth's little girl 'cause she's got fleas," William said mockingly, in a high-pitched voice, like a lady requesting prayer in a church service. Victoria and Dinky laughed almost hysterically.

"I know. She's got the worst case *I've* ever seen!" Victoria chuckled.

With that, Elizabeth let go of the fat cat. Callie Ann jumped off her shoulder and ran down the hill frantically towards Apple Muffin Cottage with the baby bonnet trailing behind her ears in the wind. Desperate for relief, Elizabeth loosened her coat collar and scratched the flea bites around her neck with both hands.

"That's the thanks I get," she said as she stomped her foot at the escaped cat. "Go on back to the house, you lazy ole fleabag!"

William, Victoria, and Dinky laughed uncontrollably while Elizabeth continued to scratch.

"Wait till Uncle J.T. and Mama hear about this," Dinky chuckled.

"My mom will crack up," added William. "Elizabeth's ate up with fleas!"

"Shut up, William Holley," replied Elizabeth, her neck still red. "Come on, let's go back," she ordered.

The little band of mourners followed her down the hill in the falling snow just as dusk was turning to night.

"I love these old clothes. Aunt Gracie said we've got to put them back in the attic before we can eat supper, though," Victoria reminded her cousin.

"Yeah, I know," Elizabeth acknowledged begrudgingly.

"You really should oil the wheels on that old thing, William." She goaded her boy cousin. The old wagon had been stored in the garage for years amidst other "important" things from bygone days, such as a very small black cast-iron pot-bellied stove, produce crates, empty apple cider bottles, and a Toledo scale used to weigh apples before they were shipped to market.

Apple Muffin Cottage

"Elizabeth, why are you so bossy?"

"Because I'm eleven and a half, and you're only eleven."

"Well, whoop-dee-do!" replied William.

Victoria, shuffling along behind, ventured again to comment, "I'm eight," to which nobody replied anything. The little girl just shrugged her shoulders and kept walking.

"Well, I'm four," chimed in Dinky cheerily, his little pug nose reddened by the cold. He stopped for a second, tilted his head backward, held onto his top hat with a loose sleeve, and caught a snowflake on his tongue.

"We all know," said Elizabeth with a slight smile, being very sisterly. Then suddenly, she stopped walking as she, too, heard the sad sound of a violin playing a familiar tune.

Shall we gather at the river

that flows by the throne of God…

"Well, that's creepy," she murmured.

"Do you hear it, too, Elizabeth?" Victoria asked. "I still

hear it. It can't just be the wind."

"Oh, come on! We're getting goofy, and I'm itchy. Let's go." Elizabeth, a bit spooked, started walking faster.

"It sounds like it's coming from the woods over by the edge of the old cemetery. Ooh! Maybe it's old Jacob Barton's ghost looking for his treasure." William acted like he was teasing, but the thought had crossed his mind.

"It's a sin to believe in ghosts!" Elizabeth shouted back at him.

"Well, didn't the legend say he played a fiddle?" Victoria reminded them.

"I'm gettin' outta here!" William yelled as he took off running. "Elizabeth's a flea-bitten, snooty-p-tooty! Last one back to the house is a rotten egg!"

"Dear Jesus, help us!" Dinky prayed desperately as he tried to run faster, holding his hat on his head with one hand while the other loose coat sleeve flapped in the wind.

The cousins fixed their eyes on the welcoming misty lights of Apple Muffin Cottage. They ran as fast as they could go across the snow-covered yard in their old floppy shoes and hats as they all heard the faint, mournful sound of a violin on the wind:

Apple Muffin Cottage

Yes, we'll gather at the river,

The beautiful, the beautiful river;

Gather with the saints at the river

That flows by the throne of God.

Chapter 4:

A Refuge from the Cold

"...because of the cold, they kindled a fire And received us all..."

Acts 28:2 (NASB)

The front door slammed shut, and the sound of loose shoes smacking on hardwood echoed from the stairwell as Elizabeth, Dinky, William, and Victoria ran up three flights of stairs, racing for the attic.

"Sounds like a herd of buffalo," J.T., who had come in for supper, said as he sat down at the kitchen table and opened the Sunday newspaper.

"Sounds like home. Just like when we were kids," said Gracie as she took a fresh apple pie out of the electric oven with a bright red mitt on each hand and placed it gently on a tile trivet in front of her brother. The room was steamy from where she had boiled potatoes. Condensation ran down the inside of the kitchen window, making a slight puddle on the wooden sill, and the humidity in the room was causing her hair to frizz.

"I just love a house full of kids," she said as she took off the oven mitts and tucked a strand of wavy strawberry-blonde hair behind one ear with a well-manicured hand. Her small diamond earrings, a wedding present from Ben, were catching light and emitting tiny sparkles with her every turn. She had thrown an old homemade cotton apron over her head earlier and tied it around her waist.

"It's a good thing you love a houseful of kids," her brother laughed as he turned to the sports section, "'cause you have one today. How you feeling, sis? You overdoing?"

"I might pay for this in the morning, but I'm enjoying myself, and the more, the merrier," Gracie said as she turned off the stove burners and the oven. "I know they're sad over Thomas Henry, though," she said, furrowing her brow with concern.

"Yeah, they always loved that old mouser, especially William."

"You liked him, too," insisted Gracie.

A Refuge from the Cold

"He sure earned his keep around the barn keepin' the rats down."

"Didn't you name those kittens? I think Elizabeth was about three when you found the two of them down by the creek. She couldn't leave them alone when we came to visit."

"Nope. Grammy named both of them. She said she would keep the little girl in the kitchen for a mouser and call her Callie Ann because she was a calico. Then said we would name the other one after Pop." J.T. folded his paper and finally looked at his sister.

"Why?" Gracie smiled, knowing Grammy had her reasons for everything and they all made sense, albeit sometimes in a roundabout way.

"She said because he was long-eared and scrawny-lookin' like Pop was when she first met him, but something about him kinda grabbed her heart. You know how she was." He smiled, and his dark eyes twinkled with delight at the memory of his grandmother. Gracie thought he was extremely handsome and found it hard to believe he was still single, but she knew the reason why, and *her* name was Patricia Dawn Meadows.

"Awe! Sweet Grammy." Gracie laughed as she piled

up fried chicken from the big iron skillet onto a serving platter.

"Hey, Gracie, did you let Marv have the old pot-bellied stove out of the garage?"

"No. Why?"

"When I was out there this morning, it wasn't there."

"Did William get it for some reason, you think?"

"Nope, he said he didn't. I asked him, and the wagon was outside the garage like somebody had been in there fooling with stuff. We should keep an eye out for strangers. The old stove pipe is missing, too. That little stove wasn't big, but it sure was heavy. Somebody had to have a way to carry it out of there, and I think I know how they did it."

"The wagon," Gracie said, a bit concerned. "I haven't seen any strangers around. Why would they take the stove and bring the wagon back?"

"Makes no sense," J.T. said.

"No, it doesn't."

"We should just keep this quiet for a while."

"Sure. No need to scare anybody." Gracie agreed.

A Refuge from the Cold

Just then, the front door flew open, hitting the wall behind it forcefully, making Gracie jump.

"Am I too late for supper?" A lively voice shouted from the living room.

"Viney always comes in so loud," Gracie remarked to her brother.

"It sure smells good in here," yelled their sister while struggling to set a large basket full of fall decorations on the sofa with gloved hands. When her grandmother was alive, Viney always decorated her house for Thanksgiving, and *by golly,* she was going to take full advantage of the opportunity to do it again now that Gracie was back and hosting the holiday this year.

"Where's Marv this evening?" J.T. asked about his brother-in-law.

"Football. Need I say more? Better give him a call; let him know I made it." LaVinia stated in abbreviated sentences as she carefully unwrapped a multicolored knit scarf from around her head and neck and pulled off her stiff leather gloves, revealing rough hands that were aged from years of gardening. She stepped back into the living room, picked up the phone, and dialed her husband.

"Hey, I'm here. Yeah, it was a little slick. I just put it in four-wheel drive and came right up the road. Nope. No problems at all. Yes, I will be careful. Love you, too. Bye."

"Is it getting colder, Viney?" Gracie asked her younger sister.

"Yes, and slick, too." LaVinia draped her coat over the back of a dining room chair and stepped into the kitchen.

Viney, so nicknamed by Pop, was the female version of him. She was taller than the average Barton woman, a bit more slender than most, too, with high cheekbones. She was earthy and liked a natural look. Therefore, she considered makeup a waste of time, but when she used a slight bit, she was beautiful by most standards. However, from a distance, her long, straight straw-colored hair and dark eyebrows gave her the slight appearance of an Afghan hound.

"Thank you. Thank you," she said, taking a hot cup of coffee Gracie handed her.

"Cream, no sugar…"

"Right. Oh, that is good, Gracie," she said after taking a long sip. "Guess what? Brotherton Arms called me today, and they want me to decorate their lobby and their conference rooms for Christmas. And I am so excited! You know that beautiful staircase in the lobby and big fireplace? To die for, right?"

"That's wonderful! Sounds like word is getting around— LaVinia Holley has the best floral designs around. Wow! That opens up a whole new area for you, kiddo. Congratulations!"

"Thank you. Makes me a bit nervous now."

"You'll do fine, and it will be beautiful!"

"No pressure there." Viney and her siblings laughed in the pleasantness of the warm kitchen.

"Supper is ready whenever we can get the kids down from the attic," Gracie said. "It reminds me of us playing up there when we were kids."

"No better place to play unless it would be the barn," added J.T. "Do you remember that rainy day out in the barn? I had that pile of corncobs I was using for batting practice, and ole Michael stepped through the barn door just as I let go with a line drive. Then *smack!*" J.T. chuckled, remembering how stunned his brother looked as he went down.

"Oh, I hated it, though," he said, trying to stifle a giggle.

"Yeah, you hated it all right," laughed Viney. "You still think it's funny after all these years. You called him Lumpy for a week because he had a big goose egg on his forehead."

"And two black eyes," added Gracie with a smile. "No wonder he became a minister—so he could pray for you."

"Well, hasn't worked yet." J.T. shrugged his shoulders.

"We'll see," Gracie smiled, knowing what Grammy knew: *The apple won't fall far from the tree. Train up a child in the way he should go, and when he is old, he won't depart from it.*

"Have you heard from Michael?" Viney asked.

"Not yet, but I think they'll be here for Thanksgiving." Gracie looked away, somewhat concerned. "And I hope Gwen and Elizabeth will get along," she added. The girls, although close in age, had never liked each other.

"By the way, how did the funeral go?" LaVinia asked.

"It wrapped up as soon as it started to snow," answered J.T.

"They're putting things away now. You should have seen William and Dinky in the old clothes and Elizabeth and Victoria in the old coats and hats. They looked so cute," added Gracie.

"I wish I could have seen them," replied Viney.

"I wish you could have, too," answered Gracie with a slight smile. "Next time."

Chapter 5:

Secrets and Treasures In the Attic

"For nothing is secret that will not be revealed, nor any thing hidden that will not be known and come to light."

Luke 8:17 (NKJV)

"Gosh, that was skeery," Dinky whimpered.

"Ole Jacob Barton, when the civil war was startin'…" William started a familiar Farmwell Valley rhyme.

"Shut up, William. You're scaring Dinky," Elizabeth demanded from him.

"Scarin' you, ya mean." William laughed as he hung Pop's old hat on a nail under the rafters.

"Scarin' me, and I ain't ashamed to admit it."

"Don't say 'ain't,' Dinky."

"Okay, Skippy, I won't."

"Should we tell somebody about it?" Victoria asked, still shaking from cold and fright.

"They'll think we're nuts and just imagining things, so…I don't know." Elizabeth was unsure. The attic got quiet. "Well, we've yakked enough."

The cousins got busy putting things away. Elizabeth re-wrapped Nancy Jane's hat in a piece of old yellowed newspaper, then put it back in the wooden trunk.

"There's so much stuff up here and in this old trunk."

"I know," Victoria agreed with her, "and all these boxes Grammy had Uncle J.T. put up here, too. Pictures. Recipes. Flower seeds. There are so many of them."

"I'd like to look through those recipes someday soon. I'd love to start a bakery one day. I'm going to start getting ready for it."

"Ooh! Bluck! I wouldn't buy anything from it if you baked stuff," William needled her.

Elizabeth ignored his rude comments as she continued to dig through the trunk.

"Look at this," she said with surprise as she picked up another old newspaper and read the headline:

NEIL ARMSTRONG WALKS ON MOON

"It's the front page of a special evening edition of the Brotherton Gazette from the first moon landing."

"Look at the date," said William, peering over her shoulder. "July 20, 1969."

"Wow," said Dinky excitedly, "that must a been a *hunderd* years ago."

"Nope, about thirty-two years ago. I know because Mom said Uncle J.T. was born on the exact same day as the moon landing. We sent him a birthday card in July before we moved here that said 'You're Out of This World' along with a box of moon pies. Remember?"

"I love moon pies." William sounded hungry.

"Uncle J.T. sure is gettin' old," said Dinky, shaking his head in dismay.

"My mom says he needs a wife, but he loves Miss Patsy, and Miss Patsy won't have much to do with him," added Victoria shyly, "even though everybody knows she loves him, too."

"Victoria, you shouldn't tell such things," her cousin scolded.

"Well, why not?" William lashed out. "Everybody knows it anyway. You're just sorry you didn't tell it, Miss Priss." He was being protective of his little sister's feelings.

"Am not, William Holley! You take that back," Elizabeth demanded of him as she stood up, put one hand on her hip, and balled up her other hand into a fist under his nose.

Her cousin waved her off, knowing she wouldn't really hit him.

"Anyway, why won't she have much to do with him?"

"'Cause he's a heathen," answered William.

"A heathen! What the heck's that?"

"A stinker," interjected Dinky as his cousins looked at him with surprise. "Mom calls me a heeven all the time, don't you remember, Elizabeth?" The little boy with the cute pug nose sat spinning around and around in an old office chair, still holding Pop's top hat on the back of his head.

"Yep, I fink it means a stinker."

"It means," added William, rolling his eyes, "that he don't believe in Jesus." A chorus of astonished gasps emanated from around the room.

"I don't believe it," said Dinky, stopping suddenly and shaking his head.

"It's awful, but it's true," said Victoria, concerned for her uncle's soul. Her bottom lip quivered, and a tear trickled down her cheek as *she* now rummaged through the old steamer trunk where she'd returned the fur muff.

"Our mom said she was mad at God for a long time when she was little because she thought he made her dad get killed in Vietnam, and that made her mom run away forever. Maybe Uncle J.T.'s mad at God," surmised Elizabeth.

"I'm not mad at God 'cause our daddy got killed, too. Are you, Elizabeth?" Dinky asked, sounding somewhat puzzled and gauging Elizabeth's reaction.

"No, Dink, I'm not," his sister said profoundly, knowing he'd never even known their dad, but she was afraid she'd worried him.

"Grammy said Romans 8:28 says that all things work

together for good to those who love the Lord and are *called according to His purpose.* And our daddy was, Dink."

"Yep, he was preachin' to the heevens, like Uncle J.T. is, down in South 'merica."

"That's right," Victoria said as she pulled a purple velvet box from the trunk that contained a miniature china tea set.

"Who's Maggie Sue O'Riley?" she asked while reading a name written on the inside lid. She was in second grade but had taught herself to read, much to her parent's amazement, before she went to kindergarten.

"I think that's our grandma," her brother answered.

"Grammy?"

"No, silly," Elizabeth whispered, "she was our great-grandma. He means the one that ran away—our Irish grandmother."

"You mean the one that rode away in a shiny red sports car—*a Corvette Convertible*—with that old hippie and ain't been heard from since?" William asked the rhetorical question while leafing through an old *Popular Mechanics* magazine he'd taken off a shelf.

"Left four little kids for Grammy and Pop to raise. And Uncle J.T. was just a newborn baby." He said with disgust.

"No wonder he's a stinker," Dinky reasoned sadly.

"How do you know all this?" Elizabeth asked while scratching her flea bites. "Besides, I thought hippies only drove Volkswagen buses with peace signs on them."

"I heard Miss Patsy's mom, that old BevAnn Meadows, talkin' about it at church once when she didn't know I was behind her. She was remembering with old Claudia Smith, who tells everything she knows. You know—telephone, telegraph, tele-Claudia, and that other gossip Linda, what's her name." He strongly disliked gossips.

"And old Claudia said our grandma was only about twenty-six at the time, with long dark red hair, and was a real looker—that's what she called her—a real looker," he continued as Elizabeth and Victoria listened intently, their eyes wide with interest.

"Does that mean a bad woman?" Victoria interrupted meekly, afraid of the answer.

"No, goof, it means pretty," Elizabeth corrected her instantly. "Now, shhh! I wanna hear the rest. Go on, William," she directed.

"Oh, sorry," her little cousin replied, blushing from the mistake.

"Anyway, I guess she walked into Hope Springs one hot summer day in 1969 wearing a pair of old cut-off blue jeans and met up with some hippie fellow at the old gas station. People'd seen him around some that summer. They said it was obvious he had money, but nobody knew much about him. He had a mustache and real long, curly blonde hair all frizzed out. Wore a leather vest and no shirt and had lots of tattoos. Old BevAnn, Claudia, and that Linda woman talked about seein' Grandma Maggie gettin' in that convertible and ridin' off with him. Both of them's long hair was blowin' in the wind, and they never looked back."

"Oh, wow," Elizabeth just couldn't believe it happened that way. "Are you sure that's what they said?"

"Said she'd probably went to Woodstock with him or back to Ireland."

"In a Corvette?" Elizabeth asked, perplexed.

"No, silly, on a plane!" William was astonished at her stupidity.

"Where's Woodstock?"

"I don't know, up in New York, I think—a big music

thing with lots of hippies."

"Poor Mommy and the rest," Victoria sighed sympathetically.

"No wonder they never talk about her," Elizabeth said.

"She's prob'ly a heeven, too," added Dinky.

"I think my mom hates her guts," William said disgustedly. "I've heard her say she'd *never* forgive her. And, if she was alive, it would *never* do for her to come back around here."

A stunned silence filled the room for a few seconds. Hate was a very strong word. Elizabeth couldn't imagine really hating someone. Although, she did strongly dislike her cousin Gwen and William at times.

"What's in here?" Dinky held up a small canvas bag with a drawstring. He found it earlier stuffed inside Pop's top hat.

"Snowman fixins!" The other kids all yelled at once.

"What in the world is *snowman fixins*?"

"It's two pieces of coal for eyes, Pop's old glasses, a pair of red wax lips, and an old corncob pipe, little cuz," William explained.

"Wow!" The little boy, who had never made a snowman before, was fascinated.

"Yeah, it's for making a snowman, Dinky," Victoria explained further.

"How do you make a snowman in a bag, Skippy?"

"It's just stuff to add to a snowman. Pop made the corncob pipe, Grammy gathered everything else up and put it in that bag, then she stuck it inside Pop's old top hat," Elizabeth said as she remembered the fun times they all had when it snowed heavily and the cousins were all at Apple Muffin Cottage together.

"So, every time we wanted to make a snowman, Grammy got the hat and pulled out this bag," Victoria added. "Then she got us a bright orange carrot from the refrigerator for a nose. We'd put on the old hat last, and the snowman almost looked real."

"Fun times making snowmen and having snowball fights," William added. "Not to mention Grammy's hot chocolate and brownies."

"Cool! I wanna do that, Elizabeth!" Dinky shouted with excitement.

"Sure, Dink. One of these days. Now, put that back on

the shelf."

"Okay, Elizabeth."

"Dink, ya better put that ole hat away, too."

"No! I'm keepin' *it*!"

"Suit yourself." Elizabeth knew when to stop insisting with Dinky. He had his mind made up.

"Fanks, Elizabeth," he said, grateful to his sister.

She looked carefully at the purple box Victoria held.

"Hey, Victoria, do you mind if I take that tea set downstairs? I remember playing with that when I was little. I'd like to show it to my mom." Fondly, she remembered Pop sitting crossed-legged on the dining room floor, drinking pretend tea out of a tiny cup with his pinky stuck out while her mom took care of newborn Dinky.

"Okay."

"Thanks, Vic."

Victoria smiled, thankful her cousin was being nice to her—almost sweet.

"There sure is a lot of old stuff up here," Elizabeth surveyed the attic again and all of the boxes Grammy had stored there.

"Who's going to go through all this?" Victoria wondered.

"I know one thing—I ain't doin' it," said William.

"Well, now, wait a minute. What if there's something up here important that Grammy wanted us to have? Or else she wouldn't have packed it up and had Uncle J.T. haul it up here. Take this box, for instance," Elizabeth read the label on top of the plastic container. "It says '**MY BEST RECIPES—TRIED AND TRUE.**'"

"Ooh, and look," said Victoria. "This box says '**ALL MY BEST SEEDS.**' Mom would definitely want these. She's been thinking about starting a nursery."

"There's all kinds of stuff up here," Elizabeth said. "I don't think we should just let it set up here and go to ruin."

"Yeah," said Victoria with tears welling up in her eyes.

"What should we do about it, then?" William asked as he cleared his throat and tried to act like he wasn't getting emotional about Grammy.

"I don't know," Elizabeth said. "Pray about it, I guess, like Grammy would. Dear Lord, please let us know what to do with all of Grammy's stuff. In Jesus' name. Amen."

"Amen," replied Dinky and Victoria.

"Come and get it!" J.T. yelled from downstairs.

"Be right there!" Elizabeth yelled back.

"Well, I'm done. Let's eat!" William shouted as he jumped up and got in front of everyone else at the top of the attic stairs. "Last one down'll be the rotten egg."

"Yeah, whatever! That's gettin' real old, William," Elizabeth said, exasperated.

"What have you kids been doing?" Gracie asked the group as they trouped into the dining room for supper.

"Havin' tea with the queen," William replied drolly as Elizabeth handed Maggie Sue O'Riley's tea set to her mother with one hand and scratched her neck with the other. Gwen always called her "Queenie," and she hated it.

"Oh, I see you found Maggie's tea set," Gracie said with a grin. "You used to play with this all the time."

"We found it in the trunk in the attic, Aunt Gracie," Victoria added.

"Well, thank you for finding it."

"You're welcome," Victoria said as she blushed again. She didn't like being the center of attention. She turned away quickly and hugged her mom.

"Hey, sweetie, how are you doin'?" Viney hugged her back.

"Fine. We found all kinds of stuff for dress up in the attic."

"I know. I used to play up there myself. It's a neat place," Viney said while Gracie motioned for everybody to sit down at the dining room table for supper.

"Why don't you kids help me go through some of those boxes that Grammy left up there? Maybe before summer?" said Gracie, recruiting some help.

"Sure," Elizabeth agreed, and all the others shook their heads yes with smiles on their faces, knowing that a prayer had just been answered.

"There's all kinds of secrets up there, too," J.T. said, seated at the head of the table, wanting to add some mystery to the attic for fun.

"Yeah, we found some seacricks up there 'bout you, Uncle J.T.," Dinky said excitedly, with his voice somewhat squeaky as he sat down at his place.

"Is that right? What'd you find up there about me?"

William and Elizabeth were holding their breath, afraid that Dinky would tell something he shouldn't. They glanced back and forth at each other, not moving their heads, only their eyes, for fear someone would know that they had been talking about J.T., Miss Patsy, Maggie Sue O'Riley, and the old hippie with the Corvette.

"We found a piece a paper up there that said you's born on the moon, and that's why you're a stinker," Dinky informed him.

The whole dining room exploded with laughter. J.T. laughed so hard he wheezed. He was so tickled he couldn't talk, and he slapped the table a couple of times and stomped his boots on the old hardwood floor.

Elizabeth laughed loudly, too, while she scratched.

"And we heard Old Jacob Barton's ghost outside when we was having Thomas Henry's funeral. He was playin' an old fiddle," Dinky told J.T.

"Yeah, 'Shall We Gather at the River,'" Elizabeth added.

"Is that right?" J.T. said as he stopped laughing. He'd heard it, too, just a little while ago.

Chapter 6:

The Mice Upstairs

"...do not be anxious about anything, but in everything by prayer and supplication with thanksgiving let your requests be made known to God."

Philippians 4:6 (ESV)

"Elizabeth, wake up. Wake up, Elizabeth. I think I heard a mouse." Dinky stood over Elizabeth in his blue and red superhero pajamas, carrying the old black top hat, waiting for her to open her eyes.

"Either a mouse or a burga-ler."

"It's just Mama going to the cellar house," Elizabeth said as she rolled over and opened one eye.

"Whew! Thought it might a been an awful big mouse. I wanna see." Dinky ran to the window that was on the right side of the old rock chimney that overlooked the side yard. "Yep, there she goes in the snow. Oh, boy! Snow!"

"Snow? Again?"

"Yep, it's pourin' it down. Will you teach me how to make a snowman, Elizabeth?" Ever since he had found the snowman fixins in the attic, it had been all he could think about.

"Can't today. Thanksgiving is Thursday. Too much to do."

"What do you have to do?"

"I need to help Mama clean the house. And besides, I have some schoolwork to do. I've been slacking off too much."

"I hate schoolwork. It's too hard."

"You don't have any schoolwork, silly!"

"Good, 'cause I wasn't gonna do it, anyways."

"Listen, Dink. Mama has lots on her plate right now. Let's help her."

"I know."

"Then help out. Don't whine. Family is coming for

Thanksgiving."

"Gwen coming, too?"

"Yes, I guess she is."

"She'll be mean to ya."

"Maybe not this time."

"She will. She'll call you Queenie and laugh at ya."

"Oh, Lord!" Elizabeth implored as she covered up her head with her blanket. "Please let Gwen be nice to me."

Chapter 7:

Gracie Ponders the Harvest

"The harvest truly is plentiful, but the laborers are few."

Matthew 9:37 (NKJV)

J.T. stepped over from the bunkhouse before dawn this morning, as usual, and fired up the old wood stove for Gracie. Snow was falling furiously, the temperature had dropped, and he didn't want the kids to be cold upstairs. She thanked him and offered him a cup of coffee and some breakfast, both of which he declined in favor of a few more hours of sleep under one of Grammy's big quilts.

"Good morning, Lord." Gracie greeted her Maker in the stillness of the morning while she waited for dawn to break. "Please help me to focus on my tasks at hand. I've got so much to do. In two days, I'll have a houseful here. What have I taken on? Please give me the strength to do this for my family. Thank You, sweet Jesus."

Her family would just have to realize that she wasn't Grammy, who had performed her well-rehearsed annual culinary feat year after year perfectly and made it look effortless. As the years rolled by, it became obvious, though, that the ravages of time on her small frame had made it harder and harder to conduct her symphony with gnarled, arthritic fingers and a stooped back.

Every Thanksgiving, no matter how she felt, she would set the big family table with her best china on her mother's prized lace tablecloth, used only for the most special occasions. Lovingly she'd place the ceramic pilgrims, known for years as John and Priscilla, center stage on the buffet. Then, just before dinner, she would let little hands feel their tiny carved faces and buckled shoes with curiosity while she told the story of the first Thanksgiving.

There were already small orange pumpkins, rust-colored candles, and dried fall flower arrangements throughout the house. LaVinia had seen to that last Sunday. Gracie loved how welcoming and festive Apple Muffin Cottage looked and smelled on holidays.

She waited for first light, then headed for the cellar house, walking carefully through the misty morning fog

Gracie Ponders the Harvest

and snow to the small, narrow footbridge that spanned Spirit Creek. She crossed it cautiously as ice-cold, gurgling water rushed nonstop beneath her, tumbling over rocks, heading downstream. Her footsteps plowed through new untouched snow as she made a path to the small building, made of logs and chinking, built into the hillside many years ago so its interior would remain a constant fifty-five degrees.

As she opened the wooden door, the rusted iron hinges creaked, and dim morning light flooded into the musty space. She turned on the flashlight she brought in her coat pocket and looked around at the partially empty room, which was a far cry from the way it used to be when bountiful treasures filled it. For years, when Spirit Creek Farm was productive and Pop and Grammy were able, they kept it full. Dozens of glass pint and quart jars sat on the hand-hewn shelves around the room, sparkling like fiery gemstones with incredible color once caught by the light. There was always yellow corn, bright red tomatoes, deep dark purple blackberries, green beans, bread and butter pickles, garlic dill pickles, apple sauce, apple butter, and a variety of other canned fruits from the orchards. The floor would also be full of baskets and crates overflowing with produce.

Grammy was always proud of her harvest, especially

all the peaches, plums, and cherries she'd picked and *put up*. But there was another harvest that concerned her more.

"Fruit for God's kingdom," she'd say. "Fruit for the kingdom. People are like fruit—handle them with lots of love and care, or they'll bruise on ya."

She said the Lord told her once when she was in the cherry orchard, "I delight in souls like you delight in this fruit, Grace. So be sure to pick up what falls to the ground. And remember, as you clean the fruit and take out the hard pits, that I cleaned you up once, too, and I took out your old stony heart and gave you a new soft one." Gracie knew that was true because Grammy had the softest heart around. Gracie smiled, thinking of her sweet grandmother.

There were a few burlap sacks full of dried black walnuts still in the shell and several baskets of apples in the corner, thanks to J.T., who had gathered what he could. It made her sad, though, to think of all the fruit that had rotted in the orchards the last few years for lack of help and, even more so, the trees that had died for lack of care.

Grammy also told her, "The Lord will always put your harvest within your reach, even though sometimes you may have to go out on a limb to get it, but He won't make it too hard for ya." Gracie thought of J.T. and had a confident

Gracie Ponders the Harvest

expectation of harvests yet to come. Grammy *had* entrusted her with all the fruit. Sometimes, she wondered about the fruit in her own life, too. Maybe Grammy was aware of her doubts.

"Lord, please help the fruit in my life be good for You and for Your glory. And the orchards. Oh, Lord, the orchards...what should I do with them? Lord, please give me Your wisdom and send me some help."

Marv and Viney were the gardeners in the family. Grammy and Pop gave them Great Aunt Belle's big rundown two-story old house, which sat just inside the city limits of Hope Springs, when they got married, along with the thirty best acres of Spirit Creek's farmland behind it. They had built a more modern addition on the back to live in, turned the first floor into a flower and gift shop, and called it Holleyhock Haven. Marv farmed the land and ran his business as a builder and contractor. Viney helped with the gardening, managed the flower shop, and did floral designs for weddings and businesses. William and Victoria helped wherever they could.

Viney's inheritance included most of the corn fields, potato fields, the hayfields behind the barn, and the woods between Apple Muffin Cottage and Holleyhock Haven. Viney's dream was to put in a nursery, have greenhouses, and raise flowers and herbs to sell. Marv had his own idea of subdividing some of the land and building houses. They were at odds, often, over what was best for the Holley family.

They'd had a good harvest this year and shared it with Gracie. Thanks to them and their hard work, they'd given her five big boxes of cabbages, two ten-pound sacks of onions, two baskets of carrots, twelve ten-pound sacks of potatoes, and six bright orange pumpkins of different sizes now setting on a large cardboard square on the dirt floor.

"Bless their hearts! But I could have sworn there were two ten-pound sacks of onions, not just one and twelve sacks of potatoes, instead of eleven and more cabbages and carrots in the baskets." A bit confused about the cellar house inventory, she continued to pick out what was needed for her Thanksgiving dinner and got back to her task at hand. She'd ask J.T. about the produce later. She had a sneaking suspicion that whoever took the stove out of the garage had also been in the cellar house and helped themselves to some food. If they'd come to the house and asked, she would have fed them gladly.

As she grabbed an empty basket from a nail on the wall and filled it with what she needed, she thought again about her grandfather and grandmother. They had farmed

Gracie Ponders the Harvest

most of their land for years with the help of just a few hired workers and their son Joshua before he died and, after that, their grandchildren.

When Spirit Creek Farm was at its peak, they grew most everything, including acres of corn, potatoes, along with apples and other fruit from their orchards. Gracie worked hard on the farm as a child, but it made her strong and confident as she grew up.

She even met her husband Ben here one summer as he helped mow the hay fields between his junior and senior years of seminary. He won her heart, made friends with her family, and helped Michael decide on his calling.

Cattle, milk cows, horses, chickens, sheep, and hogs filled up pastures, barn, pens, coops, and yard. Sometimes, even an old hound dog or two lounged on the front porch, much to Grammy's chagrin. Now, there were no animals around other than Callie Ann. The barn, coops, and pastures were empty, and so were her fields, with the exception of the orchards.

She was thankful that Marv and Viney's land was productive. J.T. was growing Christmas trees and fruit trees on his thirty acres he'd inherited, and he worked for Marv building houses. The land all seemed so disjointed.

She missed the completeness of Spirit Creek Farm.

"Lord, what happened?" Gracie suddenly felt sad and lonely. Tears trickled down her cold cheeks. It wasn't the partial emptiness of the cellar house that bothered her, or the empty barn, or the division of the farm, as much as it was the vacancies that so many of her loved ones had left—her dad, her mom, Pop, Grammy, and Ben. Now, not even Thomas Henry was here to greet her at the cellar house door. *Why had they lost so many and some so soon?* Her heart ached for them all, but she was so thankful for the loved ones she still had—her children, her siblings, and her friends.

"Thank You for all of them, Lord! I'm so thankful. And I'm so glad to be home. Please help me to take care of Your fruit like Grammy wanted me to."

After taking one last look around, she closed the heavy cellar door behind her and walked back across the footbridge carrying her basket.

Instead of a basket, Grammy always held up the corners of her apron, forming a pouch around her jars and loose produce as she made the trek back to her kitchen. Most of the time, she'd scurried back and forth with just a light sweater around her small, bent shoulders, even in the dead of winter. She'd been strong enough to withstand the cold and the wind. It was her routine for many years. It was part of her life and the way she did things. Now, Gracie would make her own routines, but Grammy's best ones she would hold onto forever. She would try to pass on the best of herself and her grandmother.

Right now, however, she had much to do and no time to waste. Ole Tom Turkey was thawing in the refrigerator.

Chapter 8:

Gracie's Memories

"Through the Lord's mercies we are not consumed, because His compassions fail not. They are new every morning; Great is Your faithfulness."

Lamentations 3:22–23 (NKJV)

The back porch was added to the house in 1922, along with two sets of stairs that had rotted and been replaced several times now over the years. Until then, a pile of three large sandstone rocks gave direct access to the back door, but with much effort. For convenience, one set of steps led down to the well and gave easier access for retrieving a bucket of water for the kitchen. However, they became obsolete in the thirties when a bright red water pump was installed at the sink itself by Thomas Barton's dad.

In the fifties, Thomas Barton installed running water in

the house for his wife Grace, making the pump an antique, left there all these years for a quaint reminder of a more laborious bygone-era. At times, it was still used to fill a large pot of water for the wood stove for various and sundry reasons.

The second set of stairs at the end of the long porch led straight up from the back path. Gracie climbed them with her arms full, being careful not to slip on the icy steps. A sign by the back door read:

> # WELCOME
> **THE BEST FOOD AROUND**

Gracie turned the old white ceramic doorknob, came into the kitchen, and sat her load from the cellar house on the counter beside the sink.

"That J.T.," she said with a chuckle, remembering that he'd painted the sign and hung it there in the late spring of 1997 when Dinky was about six weeks old.

"I'm gonna start rentin' out rooms, Grammy," she remembered J.T. saying, "'cause your house is better than a Bed and Breakfast. We'd make a fortune. People'd come from hundreds of miles around to get one of these apple muffins," he teased his elderly grandmother.

"J.T., you silly thing." Grammy's eyes twinkled as she laughed. "And you could provide entertainment, you clown. What would we call the place?" she asked while peeling apples at the kitchen table with the same paring knife she'd used for the last thirty years.

"We'll call it Apple Muffin Cottage. What else?" Pop interjected as he shuffled through the kitchen door that morning. He grinned and winked at Grammy, knowing how proud she was of her prizewinning muffins, which were famous for years all over Farmwell Valley. "That's what everybody calls it anyway—all your customers—all the time. 'Let's call up Apple Muffin Cottage and order us some of those good muffins.'"

The memory of that day made Gracie smile. She was glad for the sign by the back door that jogged her memory. She missed the grandparents that had raised her and her sister and two brothers. In ways, it was like they were still here. They were so much a part of her she knew exactly what they would say.

"Now, Gracie," Grammy would have said, "get that wet jacket off and come get ya a cup of coffee and sit down and talk to me."

I'd love to, Grammy.

"Missy," Pop always called her, "don't you worry about those kids because they're going to be just fine."

I know, Pop.

But it wasn't that way with her dad or Maggie. She had forgotten them long ago. Just parts of them lingered with her there in Apple Muffin Cottage. She remembered being five years old on a hot August day and asking her mother to show her the diamonds in the snow again someday like she had done the Christmas before when the moon shone on the white fields and made them sparkle. Maggie promised she would before kissing her on top of the head and leaving out the front door, never to return. Gracie watched her walk off the front porch, crunch through the dry grass in the yard past the grape arbor, walk through the gate, then turn left onto the old dirt road.

Without thinking, she reached for the familiar purple box on the kitchen table beside her laptop. She opened it carefully, knowing it contained the miniature tea set that was her mother's. Gracie herself had played with it many times as a child. Even in the dark of night, she could always picture the pink roses and blue and purple pansies

Gracie's Memories

hand painted on the delicate china—each piece trimmed in gold with royal blue handles.

Lovingly, she touched the name written on the inside of the lid in large childlike scrawl as if she were touching the face of her mother and wondering, once again, like she had done for the last thirty-two years, if she were alive or dead.

"Why don't we look for her, Grammy?" Gracie asked her grandmother many times through the years.

Grammy's reply would always be the same. "Best to leave it to the good Lord."

Suddenly, in her mind, she was able to see the outline of her mother with the summer sun shining brilliantly behind her, giving her an aura resembling that of an angelic being in a white cotton dress. Gracie remembered her often this way, but she had lost the memory of her mother's face long ago. Try as she might, she couldn't retrieve it.

"Let's have our tea party picnic here under the apple trees," she could still hear her mother say with a thick Irish accent. "We have a lot to celebrate. Grammy, show us your blue ribbon you won at the fair yesterday for your apple muffins."

Apple Muffin Cottage

A much younger Grammy shyly held up a blue ribbon. Maggie applauded her mother-in-law's triumph. A taller, more square-shouldered Pop, sitting in a lawn chair, stood up, bowed, and tipped his black hat at his wife as if she were the queen of England. It was a prized possession given to him when he was a boy by a circus ringmaster for helping water the elephants during a stop at Hope Springs Station.

It must have been late summer of 1968. J.T. wasn't born yet. Michael, Gracie's other brother, was only two that summer, and Viney was about six months old, lying in an old wicker laundry basket on a pillow. Gracie herself was just four, but she remembered how happy they all were that beautiful day. Since then, she had never seen a sky as blue or clouds so white and fluffy.

"And the best news of all," Grammy said excitedly to the little ones seated on a table cloth on the ground in the orchard, "is that your daddy will be home in October and gets to stay for Thanksgiving this year." Her round face was shining with joy, and a brilliant, broad smile showed off pearly white teeth and deep, dimpled cheeks. Everybody, except Viney, of course, cheered and clapped their hands.

Her dad must have come home in October that year because J.T. was born the next summer. She didn't remember seeing him for the last time before he left for Vietnam, but she remembered how good he smelled and how strong his hands were when he picked her up and kissed her cheek. A sure feeling of love and security swept over her, and she remembered how much her dad loved her.

"Some good memories," Gracie said out loud. She'd have to let the kids have a tea party soon. It was a shame that the Regal Brookshire had not been used for so long now. Grammy had put it away in the trunk upstairs for safekeeping, where Victoria found it. Gracie touched each piece tenderly, knowing that her mother's small hands had played with them when she was a child in Ireland. As she turned the box over, she realized again that Grammy had taped a yellow post-it note to the bottom on which she had written "Timeless Treasures—Dublin." It *was* a timeless treasure.

Gracie got lost in thought, standing in the dim morning light of the kitchen.

"Maggie Sue O'Riley," she said out loud before she replaced the lid on the box and scooted it out of the way, "where are you?"

How could you have left us, Maggie? The question was always on her mind. At times, feelings of rejection and abandonment haunted her.

Grammy's kitchen, now hers, was always so inviting. Today, it was a warm retreat from the cold November weather. Callie Ann, wearing her new flea collar, thought so too as she curled up on a braided rug in front of the old wood stove.

The familiar copper tea kettle whistled and jolted Gracie out of her daydream. She grabbed a tea bag from a small canister atop a shelf next to the kitchen window. All she needed now was a cup and saucer from Grammy's cupboard and an apple muffin from the warming drawer. She was going to spread it thick with real butter and enjoy it with her Darjeeling tea. She had to remember it was her cupboard now, her cups and saucers, her Apple Muffin Cottage. She was adjusting to it slowly, but for now, Gracie wanted to sit down and savor this quiet, early morning moment before the day took a hectic turn, as it usually did.

"Dear Lord, thank You for this food. Bless it and give me strength for the day," she prayed with her head bowed and hands folded over her breakfast. "Please continue to bless my children and me. Help us to bear good fruit for You. In Christ's name, I pray. Amen." It had been difficult for her to pray the last few years at her table in the city, in her apartment, but somehow, now that she was here,

Gracie's Memories

praying seemed to come a little easier at Grammy's kitchen table.

Although it was Tuesday and a school day, the kids were still asleep (she thought). Dinky wouldn't start kindergarten until next fall, and she was home-schooling Elizabeth this year in order to ease her through the transition. Her beautiful but somewhat haughty young daughter didn't mind, and neither should the unsuspecting souls at Hope Springs Elementary School if they knew what was good for them. She was hoping that Elizabeth could be humbled a bit by Spirit Creek Farm life before mixing much with other Farmwell Valley children and before starting middle school next fall.

Elizabeth had assumed more of an adult role after the death of *her* father, Gracie's husband, Ben. She took charge at home while Gracie was working. It was an act of control that made it hard to keep babysitters. Over the years, her little girl had become a caretaker. She cleaned house and learned how to cook at an early age and helped mother Dinky. Gracie had done the same thing in her childhood after her dad's plane went down in Vietnam and Maggie ran away. Being the oldest, she felt responsible for the younger children and tried to fill a void.

As Gracie worked and her health worsened, she saw

her daughter take on more and more responsibility until she knew things had to change for all their sakes. They had to get away from Brotherton. The school there had become a cruel place for Elizabeth, primarily because of Gwen.

The new routine seemed to be working really well for all of them on Spirit Creek Farm since they'd moved there in late summer. She and Elizabeth both were more relaxed, but still, she would like to see a softer heart in her daughter and better *fruit*.

"Show me a young widowed woman under a lot of stress with children and a career, who is an overachiever anyway, and I'll show you a woman with fibromyalgia. And you've just lost your grandparents, for heaven's sake! Girl, you are not invincible. You are actually very fragile. How much more can you take?" Dr. Barnes knew what was wrong when she started having odd aches and pains and strange fatigue she couldn't explain.

"I delivered you, and I've known you all your life, kiddo. You're at a breaking point, I hate to say. You need to make some lifestyle changes before you're forced to," he warned her sternly. "You need fresh air, lots of sleep, sunshine, and time with your children."

Gracie remembered saying to him, "I have kids to

raise, Doc, and how I'm going to do that without a job? Although, I do have Ben's life insurance money I was holding on to and my 401k."

"And you have Apple Muffin Cottage."

"Okay, Doc, you win." She had mixed emotions about giving up her career as a computer specialist but looked forward to being a full-time mom to Elizabeth and Dinky.

So, she traded in her BMW for a four-wheel drive Jeep. Now, every time they crossed Spirit Creek, she'd yell, "Hey, kids, we're crossing the creek! Hold up your feet!" just like Pop used to do, and they obliged her every time, pretending like they were keeping their feet dry. What once seemed impossible was now a reality. They'd moved out of their apartment and were living in their own house, Apple Muffin Cottage, back on the farm, healing, breathing, praying, and enjoying *the little things*. Maybe now she could even put Maggie to rest.

She could hear Grammy's voice in her mind saying to her once more, "Enjoy the little things in life 'cause the big things may never come along."

While she continued to sip her tea and finish her muffin, she enjoyed a few minutes of relaxation, wistfully gazing past the red and white curtains through the old window that framed her rolling hills and meadows, now white with new snow. A feeling of complete contentment came over her, along with a sense of really being at home, and the weight of the world was off her shoulders.

"Thank You, Lord," she whispered.

"Um. These muffins are really good," she remarked to a sleeping Callie Ann after tasting another bite. "I'll have to remember to compliment Elizabeth. Grammy sure taught her well."

The prayer and the warm, delicious breakfast *hit the spot*. She'd be ready for the day's challenges after she made a quick store list for J.T. Callie Ann began to stir, stood up, stretched, then laid back down, curling up in a tight ball. Her place by the stove was just too warm and cozy to leave.

"I know how you feel, girl," Gracie chuckled, "I know just how you feel."

She made the dial-up connection on her laptop and checked her email.

No new messages.

Gracie opened the purple box and looked at her mother's name again inside the lid, put her fingers on the laptop keys, and pulled up a search engine. Stealthily, on a whim, she quickly typed in *Maggie Sue O'Riley*, held her breath, and hit the enter button.

"Oh, dear Lord, *You have got to be kidding me!*" Gracie gasped as she read what had appeared on her screen but what she really hadn't expected:

TIMELESS TREASURES

Maggie Sue O'Riley, Appraiser of Fine China—New York, New York, previously Dublin, Ireland

> *I buy and sell, give online valuations, sell on consignment, give helpful tips on how to care for your fine china and porcelain...*

"Oh, it couldn't be!" Gracie continued to read, her heart pounding. *It couldn't be her Maggie. It just couldn't. How had Grammy known about Timeless Treasures in Dublin?*

Gracie clicked on the website. There was a place for posting questions. There was also an email address listed. She copied it; she would bypass the web page where postings were visible to everyone. In the body of an email, she wrote:

> *I am interested in the value of an antique miniature Regal Brookshire tea set circa 1950. Can you help me?*
>
> Mrs. B. D. LeMaster

She quickly hit the send button before losing her nerve. Surely, this couldn't be her mother. After all, her name would be Maggie Sue Barton. Why would she be using her maiden name? But Grammy somehow knew about *Timeless Treasures*. How and why?

She wouldn't mention this to the others right now, especially not to Viney.

Chapter 9:

Miss Patsy Stops by with the "Seacrick" Ingredient

"But the fruit of the Spirit is love, joy, peace, longsuffering, kindness, goodness, faithfulness, gentleness, self-control."

Galatians 5:22 (NKJV)

Recipe: *Pumpkin Pie Filling*

2 eggs

3/4 c. brown sugar firmly packed

1 (15 ounce) can 100% pure pumpkin

1/2 teaspoon salt

1-3/4 teaspoons pumpkin pie spice

1 (12 fluid ounce) can of evaporated milk

1 generous helping of Grammy's secret ingredient (love)

"Whatcha doin', Elizabeth?" Dinky asked as he lifted up the spice container and took a decided sniff. "Smells good. Is this Grammy's seacrick gredient?"

"Dinky LeMaster, keep out of things! You are so annoying," whined Elizabeth, still gorgeous even with a dusting of flour on her small upturned nose. Her auburn hair was pulled back at the nape of her neck with a scrunchy, and curly loose strands of it fell around her delicate oval face.

Miss Patsy Stops by with the "Seacrick" Ingredient

"I just wanna know. Is this Grammy's seacrick gredient?"

"No."

"Then what is it?" he whimpered.

"It's pumpkin pie spice. It goes into pumpkin pies and makes them taste good." Elizabeth explained, a little more patient than she was before. After all, Dinky could get on her nerves, but she hated to hurt his feelings. He could look so cute sometimes when he whined pitifully and tilted his head to one side. He definitely got his smattering of freckles and hair from their mother, but he *was* the spitting image of their dad.

"But what is the seacrick gredient? Everybody always said that Grammy put some in everything she made. You put it in yours, too, Elizabeth?"

"No, Dink, I don't. You're bothering me. Put that old thing away," she demanded, pointing to his latest obsession, the black hat, worn threadbare in places and carried upside down, filled with small cars and plastic circus animals.

"Why do you always carry that ole thing around? It's dirty, and you're dirty."

"It was Pop's, and I miss Pop."

"You don't even remember Pop."

"Yes, I do too! He used to wear this old hat sometimes. Once, he told me I could have it."

"But you weren't even one when he died. Oh…never mind! Whatever. Just don't get next to my pie filling." Elizabeth rattled off orders to her little brother drill-sergeant-style while continuing to pat her pie crust into the second of two beautiful glass pie plates that Grammy always used for special occasions. She trimmed the uneven edges of raw store-bought dough around the pie plate with a small paring knife and determined the second one would look better than the first. The other, sitting on the table waiting for filling, looked okay but not up to her true standards.

The edges on the crust had to be pinched just right like Grammy taught her. She needed to concentrate. The kitchen was too hot because of the heat from the electric oven and the wood stove. It was making her tense, so she stopped what she was doing and opened the backdoor to let some cool air into the kitchen before continuing.

Cautiously, she placed the forefinger and thumb of her left hand on the outside edge of the pie dough, pinched it slightly, then pressed in between them with the forefinger

Miss Patsy Stops by with the "Seacrick" Ingredient

of her other hand. She would attempt to repeat this process until the circumference of the single crust was uniformly indented.

Dinky stood by her elbow, watching pensively, his dirty fingernails tapping on the table. "Elizabeth, when we get to heaven, will we have wings and a helmet?" he asked with genuine curiosity, catching Elizabeth off guard.

"What in this world are you talking about?" At this point, she stopped what she was doing, wiped her hands on her apron, and looked at Dinky.

"Wings and a helmet? Where did that come from?"

"If Grammy gots a halo, then Daddy must a gotta helmet. Right? Only girl angels gots halos. I don't wanna halo. When I get to heaven, I wanna helmet like football guys gots."

Elizabeth had a confused look on her face. For a moment, in her mind, she pictured Dinky with angel wings on his back and a football helmet on his head.

"Dink, you shouldn't be worried about stuff like that. You're too little, and we shouldn't even be thinkin' about it."

"Wonder what Thomas Henry gots? A tiny little helmet on top of his little head, I bet," Dinky grinned.

"Imagine that. Thomas Henry with a helmet," Elizabeth chuckled.

"And don't furget," Dinky said, giggling, "he prob'ly gots tiny little wings, too."

"Dink, you are too funny," his sister laughed, continuing to flute the edge of her pie crust, turning it around as she went.

Elizabeth eyed her second masterpiece. "Wonderful. Now, I can pour in the filling."

"Did you put in the seacrick gredient?"

"Dinky, I told you…" Elizabeth stopped when she heard someone at the door.

"Knock. Knock. Can I come in?"

"Miss Patsy, hi! Sure, come on in," Elizabeth smiled and motioned to her guest to step into the kitchen. She thought the world of Miss Patsy.

"Hi, Elizabeth, and hey there, Dinky. How've you been? I was sorry to hear about Thomas Henry," Miss Patsy rattled off her salutation. She was a pretty woman, about thirty-one, with a healthy, just slightly athletic build. Her lovely oval face, framed by her long blonde hair, was

Miss Patsy Stops by with the "Seacrick" Ingredient

creamy and flawless. When she smiled, her blue eyes twinkled with joy, and she seemed to always be filled with light.

"Oh, I like your hair! You straightened it. It's pretty. Mama and I should straighten ours sometime."

"I'm glad you like it. Thank you, Elizabeth." Patsy ran her left hand through her hair. Her hands and her voice were very elegant. She was the church choir director, the youth choir leader and taught voice lessons out of her and her mom's home. Her mom was the church pianist and taught piano out of their home, as well. Everyone laughingly called it "Melody Manor" because it was the music center of Hope Springs.

Patsy also worked in her mom's grocery store, ordering stock, paying bills, and generally doing what needed to be done. If anybody knew her, they also knew that she loved Jesus, J.T. Barton, music, and lighthouses. J.T. had even asked her to marry him about ten years ago, but she turned him down. Some said that it was because he wasn't a Christian. Others speculated it was because her mother, BevAnn, hated the Barton family, with the exception of Grammy and Pop, and would never have stood for it. Many said it was because she wanted a music career.

Shortly after the thwarted proposal, she *did* head to Nashville but was back in two years, having not "made it" in country music—mainly because she couldn't and wouldn't compromise her beliefs. J.T. never asked her again for fear of rejection, but he knew he'd never love anybody else like he loved Miss Patricia Dawn Meadows.

"Thomas Henry's in heaven now, Miss Patsy. And he gots tiny little wings and a little helmet, I bet," Dinky nodded.

"A helmet? You think?" Miss Patsy couldn't keep from smiling at the adorable little boy as she looked into his big blue eyes. Dinky always made her smile.

"Prob'ly," Dinky affirmed.

"Well, I wouldn't doubt it at all," Miss Patsy said, giving Elizabeth a quick wink.

"Where's your mom?" Gracie and Patsy had been good friends for years.

"She and Uncle J.T. went to the barn to get some tulip bulbs that Aunt Viney gave her to set out by the front porch. It's November, you know—time to plant tulip bulbs." Elizabeth shared her knowledge but noticed that Miss Patsy seemed disappointed that J.T. or Gracie weren't around.

Miss Patsy Stops by with the "Seacrick" Ingredient

"Yes, it is. I set some out at our house last week. I caught a real nice day to do it. I put them out along the front walkway. They ought to be real pretty come next spring. My mom and some of the other ladies from church set out a few bulbs in the church flower bed, too, and around the lamp posts."

"That's nice." Elizabeth thought that probably Claudia and some of the other church gossipers had been the ones to help plant the bulbs. They always seemed to be hanging around Miss Patsy's mom. Where one of them went, the others seemed to follow. They reminded her of a gaggle of honking geese—just making noise to let everyone know they were there and it was *their* territory.

Miss BevAnn Meadows owned Meadows' Grocery, which was the only store in town, and she'd inherited that from her father. She'd never been married, never even dated, as far as the townspeople knew. Consequently, Miss Patsy's paternal beginnings were a great mystery to all, including Miss Patsy herself.

BevAnn left Hope Springs in late 1969 to study music in Salzburg, Austria, for a few months. She came back in the early summer of 1970 with a two-month-old baby. BevAnn never gave any explanations, and no one in Hope Springs dared to ask. All anyone ever knew was that she'd had an adorable baby girl that everybody loved.

She was also head of the Church Beautification Committee, as well as the Ladies Aid Society. There wasn't much in Hope Springs that she wasn't in charge of, including Miss Patsy herself. Which may have contributed (some have surmised) to Miss Patsy being a self-professed *old maid*. But Elizabeth knew she loved her uncle J.T. and that there was nobody else that Miss Patsy would ever marry either.

"I bet those tulips will be pretty, too," Elizabeth added politely.

"I'm sure they will be. Uh, sweetie, the check-out boy forgot to put this smaller bag in your uncle J.T.'s grocery bag yesterday, and I figured your mom might need it for cooking, so I thought I'd drop it off on my way out the road. I have to make a delivery to Mr. Tabor. Will you make sure Gracie knows I dropped it off?"

"Sure I will," she said, thinking she'd let Uncle J.T. know, too.

"What's in there?" Dinky asked, looking into the small brown paper bag.

"It's a secret." Miss Patsy whispered as she grinned

Miss Patsy Stops by with the "Seacrick" Ingredient

and patted Dinky on the nose with one finger.

Ring. Ring. The ringing telephone in the living room startled Elizabeth.

"Oh, I'd better get that, Miss Patsy, since Mom's not here. I'll see you later." Elizabeth ran to the living room, her fuzzy purple house slippers flopping on the floor as she went.

"Happy Thanksgiving, Elizabeth," Miss Patsy called to her.

"You too, Miss Patsy. Hello. Oh, hello, Dr. Barnes. No, she's out right now. May I take a message?"

"Well, Dinky, I'd better go. You have a happy Thanksgiving, too. Don't you eat too much turkey. And I'll see you in Sunday school." Miss Patsy also taught four and five-year-olds on Sunday mornings.

"Bye, Miss Patsy, I won't," Dinky said obligingly as she left. Once again, he peeked curiously into the brown paper bag…

Chapter 10:

Thanksgiving at Apple Muffin Cottage

"Enter into His gates with thanksgiving and into His courts with praise."

Psalm 100:4 (NKJV)

On Thanksgiving morning, Elizabeth woke up to the smell of roasting turkey filling Apple Muffin Cottage. Her experienced "sniffer" also detected a hint of Grammy's homegrown sage that her mom had picked from the herb bed and dried in late summer for cornbread stuffing to fill Ole Tom Turkey.

Gracie readied him last night before she went to bed, then set her alarm for 4:00 a.m. to put him in the oven. She rinsed, patted dry, and salted him inside and out. Then, she stuffed, trussed his wings and legs tightly with kitchen twine, and smeared him entirely with butter before tucking him neatly into the roasting pan. Her performance drew an audience of three—J.T., Elizabeth, and Dinky—who all marveled at her expertise. They had all taste-tested the stuffing while it was still in her largest white ceramic mixing bowl and declared that it was "almost" as good as Grammy's.

"What size bird is that?" J.T. asked Gracie while she was basting the turkey. His voice, along with the stove's heat, carried up from the kitchen through a vent in Elizabeth's bedroom floor, and she could hear their conversation. Pop cut out the vent years ago to keep his granddaughters warm in their bedroom by letting the hot air from the wood stove continue to rise upward.

"About a twenty-pounder, and I hope he's as good as he looks," answered Gracie.

"He sure smells good." J.T. inhaled deeply.

"Well, as Grammy would say, 'the proof's in the puddin'.'"

"Right," J.T. concurred.

"How 'bout a cup of coffee and a piece of pumpkin pie to go with it? I haven't had breakfast yet." J.T. was accustomed to having a piece of Grammy's pumpkin pie for breakfast every Thanksgiving morning for most of his life, and he had missed it the last few years.

"Don't you dare cut my pies, Uncle J.T.!" Elizabeth yelled down through the vent.

"Well, why not, Bethie?" J.T. was sharply disappointed by the refusal.

"They're special, 'at's why," yawned Dinky as he walked into the kitchen in his pajamas, his hair sticking out in several different directions, carrying Pop's old hat. "Happy Fanksgivin, Mom. I smell Ole Tom Turkey."

"Good morning, sunshine. Happy Turkey Day. I laid your clothes out on your bed. Go get yourself dressed for Mom," Gracie reached out and gave Dinky a hug.

"Oka-ay. Do I gots to comb my hair and brush my teeth, too?"

"Yep, sure do. J.T., get a piece of that apple cake. Elizabeth made the pumpkin pies, and she wants to show them off."

"Well, I guess I can wait. How 'bout a piece of that black walnut cake?" J.T. raised one eyebrow and grinned at Gracie in anticipation.

"Oh, okay," Gracie relented. She had really wanted to put it in the center of the dessert table because it looked so pretty. It had cream cheese frosting loaded with black walnuts, and it was three layers high. "Elizabeth's pies will take center stage this year anyway. Look how pretty they are." She was proud that Elizabeth was such an accomplished baker.

"Who all's coming today, Gracie?" J.T. held a plate out to her for a piece of cake, which she cut carefully and thinly.

"There should be an even dozen of us if Dr. Barnes comes. I invited him, but I haven't heard anything."

"Oh, Mom, I forgot to tell you. Dr. Barnes called and said he'd be here." Elizabeth shouted from her room.

"An even dozen, then." Gracie was glad he was coming. There was no need for him to be alone today.

"Elizabeth," Gracie yelled towards the ceiling, "I could use your help."

"Be down in a minute, Mom," Elizabeth shouted back her answer while smoothing her hair in front of the oval mirror above her dresser. She glanced down at a picture of Maggie and Joshua that she'd found in the old desk situated underneath the window in her room. She hadn't told her mom that she had found it. Maybe she wouldn't. She didn't want to upset her, especially not today. Elizabeth thought she definitely looked like her grandmother. Their faces *were* quite similar, as well as their hair. The photo revealed the same creamy complexion, full lower lip, and emerald green eyes. She touched her finger to Maggie's face. She definitely *was* a looker.

She found herself a little melancholy today. Memories of Thanksgivings past with her dad were fading away, but she could still remember Grammy and Pop. If she was not careful, she would cry this morning, and she didn't want anyone to see her cry.

So she straightened her shoulders and threw back her head, took a deep breath, and headed downstairs with an ache in her heart but began to sing.

Shall we gather at the river

where bright angel feet have trod?

She sang determinedly, always looking forward to that blessed hope of heaven and being reunited with her great-grandparents and her dad again someday.

Gracie smiled when she heard Elizabeth singing the song that had been sung at all three funerals—Ben's, Pop's, and Grammy's. She knew that her daughter was missing all of them today, as was she, and she was proud of her for being strong.

Elizabeth got busy and set the dining room table even though her heart was heavy. She was taking Grammy's advice—stay busy because idle hands are the devil's workshop and put on a garment of praise for the spirit of heaviness because God inhabits our praises.

A whole flood of memories had been flowing through Gracie's mind, too. Her thoughts, naturally, drifted back to Maggie. If she was alive, did she have another family? Where had she been the last thirty-two Thanksgivings? It was a wild and inconceivable idea, but maybe, just maybe, someday she'd be back at Apple Muffin Cottage with her children and grandchildren.

As she peeled sweet potatoes at the kitchen sink, she remembered another Thanksgiving a few years back when she, along with LaVinia and Michael's wife Alice, were all expecting their first babies. When they tried to help with dinner, they realized they couldn't all fit into the kitchen.

Thanksgiving at Apple Muffin Cottage

They were turning sideways and squeezing past each other when Pop got tickled and shouted to Grammy, "Look here, Grace! Whales are trying to beach themselves in our kitchen."

Joining in on the joke, Grammy yelled back at him, "Thomas! You leave those poor fat girls alone!" The whole house rang with laughter, everyone knowing that Grammy herself was the roundest of all. Gracie chuckled out loud at the memory.

"What's so funny?" J.T. asked, reaching around her to put his cake plate into the sink.

"Oh, just thinking about good times."

"There'll be more to come, Gracie." J.T. bent over and gave his sister a quick kiss on top of the head.

"I know," she said, her voice breaking somewhat with emotion. She wanted so badly to tell him about Maggie, but she would wait until she had definite proof. Either way, it might not be welcome news.

After J.T. left the kitchen, Gracie took the time to check her email again.

No new messages.

"Mom, why does Gwen hate me?" Elizabeth asked Gracie as she came into the kitchen.

"Well, I don't think she hates you. I think you two just clash. Your personalities are so different."

"Well, I think she hates me, and I don't know why," Elizabeth persisted. "I'm not going to have anything else to do with her."

"What does Jesus say in the Bible about loving our enemies?" Gracie knew the answer, but she wanted to remind Elizabeth.

"To love them, and if they are hungry, feed them. If they are thirsty, give them something to drink. And pray for them."

"That's right," said Gracie, "and in so doing, we are more like Him."

"But Gwen is a PK. She should know how to be nice," Elizabeth interjected.

"A PK?" Gracie looked quizically at Elizabeth.

"You know. A preacher's kid."

"Oh," Gracie smiled. "Well, none of us are perfect. Just try to be nice to her. Because you are one, too, ya know."

"What? Oh, a PK. I guess so. I forgot," Elizabeth giggled. "I'll try, but if she or William call me 'Queenie' one more time..."

"You'll what?" Gracie waited for her answer with a raised eyebrow.

"I'll try to be nice," relented Elizabeth.

"Thank you," said Gracie. "We're known by our fruit, you know. Grammy used to say, 'Sometimes really pretty people are like a real pretty red apple all shiny and polished on the outside, but when you cut it open, it's rotten on the inside.'"

"God sees what's inside our hearts, Bethie. So take care and don't let unforgiveness or resentment make you rotten. Okay?"

"Okay, Mom, okay."

"Dinky, who's at the door?" Gracie hoped it was Michael and his family when the doorbell rang. They were late, and she was anxious.

The Thanksgiving smells were wonderful and filled the whole house with the wonderful aroma of hot rolls, turkey with sage stuffing, cranberry salad, mashed potatoes and gravy, and desserts fit for kings. Gracie was worn out but happy and proud that everyone was gathering at Apple Muffin Cottage again for the first time since Grammy passed away.

"Hey, it's Dr. Barnes with John and Priscilla and their kid," answered Dinky.

"What?" Gracie stepped through to the living room to see what he was talking about. "Hey, Doc. Hey, everybody! Welcome! Happy Thanksgiving! Come on in." Dr. Barnes patted her as she gave him a quick hug.

"Looks like the pilgrims have landed," he said laughingly as he went on past the others into the dining room.

"Hey, Gracie, it smells great in here!" Her brother Michael greeted her in full pilgrim attire. "We just came over on the Mayflower and didn't have time to change. Sorry, we're late." He made a fine-looking pilgrim with his tall hat, black shirt with a big white collar, knee breeches, and white knee socks with big buckled shoes as he leaned in to hug his sister.

"Is this the latest fashion for clergy and their families these days?" Gracie laughed and hugged Michael back. "It's good to see you. So glad you're here!"

"Hey, Gracie, don't we look silly? We had a Thanksgiving dinner at church last night for the less fortunate, and we did a little skit. We wanted to show you our costumes," added her sister-in-law Alice, always bubbly, as she hugged Gracie, too.

"How cute! You did a good job on these."

"Gwen and I made them together last week at the fabric shop. Michael has been so busy we decided to busy ourselves, too."

"And Gwen, how are you?" Gracie said as she patted the girl's arm. She always tried to pay attention to her niece, even though, most of the time, the attention was not wanted.

"Fine," answered the young girl very curtly. She was wearing a long black dress with a huge white collar. Gracie quickly stifled a giggle as she saw Gwen looking forlorn with a white bonnet tied under her chin and her coarse dishwater-blonde hair sticking out from around it, framing her square face. Her piercing blue eyes squinted in defiance and humiliation. There was nothing feminine yet or delicate about her. She reminded Gracie of Alice's late father, the former *hellfire and brimstone* pastor of Hope Springs Church, Reverend Alfred Finney, who was a big, burly man with a loud, booming voice that always scared babies and little kids.

"Gwen, I wanna tell you something. It's a seacrick," said Dinky as he pulled his cousin off to the side. He was whispering something to her, and she seemed to be very interested in what he had to say.

"Hey, Gwen," Elizabeth greeted her, resolving to be gracious but quietly disgusted that her cousin would allow herself to look so ridiculous.

"Hey, Queenie," said Gwen, seizing the opportunity to tease Elizabeth and to get the attention off herself. "Did you do any of the cooking?"

Elizabeth cautiously nodded her head. "I made the pumpkin pies." Gwen was up to something. She just knew it.

"Come and eat," yelled J.T. from the dining room, where some of the others were already being seated. Gracie had just set the last dish on the table—candied sweet potatoes.

"Well, whoop-dee-doo, Queenie," whispered her obnoxious cousin. "This should be interesting—real interesting."

"Hey, Cuz's!" Gwen waved to William and Victoria, who were already seated at the kids' section of the table.

"Hey," William answered and waved back.

"Hi, Gwen," Victoria acknowledged her cousin cautiously because of the way she'd always teased and tormented Elizabeth. She didn't approve and hoped she'd never be on the receiving end of Gwen's wrath.

Elizabeth sat down, and then Gwen squeezed into the seat next to her before Dinky could.

Viney brought in a pitcher of iced tea, while Gracie brought in the hot rolls. Then, all of the adults were seated, too. Viney's decorations were beautiful on top of Grammy's lace tablecloth that covered the one-hundred-year-old table. Earlier, Elizabeth had set the table with Grammy's good china and her stemmed glassware. She remembered what Grammy taught her as she laid down the silverware at each place: fork on the left and knife and spoon on the right.

"Michael, would you bless the food for us?" Gracie asked her brother.

"Sure. Dear heavenly Father, we are so thankful today for all that You've given us, especially salvation through the cross of Calvary. Please bless this food and the hands that have prepared it. Thank You for those loved ones who've gone on before us and who we miss so much today. And, Lord, wherever Maggie is, please let her know we still love her. Help us all to forgive her as You've forgiven us. In the precious name of Jesus, we pray. Amen."

Viney cleared her throat. "Wow, that's a first, Michael." She had vowed never to forgive her mother for abandoning them. "Easier said than done." Marv slipped his arm around her as if to shield her from the mention of her mother.

"I think that's the first time I've ever heard Maggie's name mentioned at Thanksgiving before," Gracie added as she wiped a tear from her cheek. Alice grabbed a napkin and dabbed at her eyes.

"Well, I just feel like it's time…" Michael said nervously.

"Let's eat! Pass that turkey, Michael," J.T. said in order to change the subject. He'd been hungry for it ever since he'd sliced it and had a bite or two.

"I'm all for that," Doc Barnes laughed. "I'm hong-ree!"

Dinner was a complete success. Even Gracie's hot rolls

turned out light and fluffy.

"Doc, please have seconds," Gracie encouraged her dear friend.

"No, I don't believe I will. I'm working on my figure," he said as he patted his round belly. "This won't look very good on the beach in Florida."

"When ya leavin' us, Doc?" Marv asked the aging doctor with sincere interest.

"I'm heading out next week. My apartment is ready and waiting. It's one of those senior places where they come in and make your bed for you, and they have a cafeteria. Won't have to cook for myself anymore. And it's one block over from the beach. And there's a pool."

"Very nice, Doc. We're glad for you, but we're really going to miss you," Michael said.

"I'm going to miss all of you, but I'm so tired of these *dasted* cold winters." He knew better than to really cuss in Apple Muffin Cottage and especially at Grace Barton's table.

"Well, you stay warm, Doc. You've certainly earned that privilege." Viney was glad that he was finally getting to retire.

"You kids have been the closest thing to family I've ever had. So, please, come see me from time to time."

"We will, Doc, and we'll be checking in on you regularly," Viney said, her voice breaking a little as she leaned over and gave the white-haired old man a kiss on the cheek. He looked so small to her now. There were times during her childhood, especially when she had to have a shot, that he looked like a giant to her. She remembered his coal-black hair and bright blue eyes twinkling at her as he handed her a pack of chewing gum at the end of every office visit.

"Your new doctor will be here after the first of the year. Brotherton General assures me he's Board Certified, and he really wants to be here. His name's Ian McVicker. Some folks call him Dr. Mac."

"Who?" Gracie jumped with surprise.

"Ian McVicker. Do you know him?"

"Well, yes, I do," Gracie said as she blushed. "He was the plant doctor at Brotherton Alloys."

"I hear he's single and real good-looking," Dr. Barnes smiled, winked, and tried to gauge Gracie's reaction.

"I wouldn't know," Gracie fibbed out of embarrassment.

The truth was, she did know. She had been out to dinner with him twice. She thought he was very attractive, and there had been a definite spark between the two of them; however, she had been too sick and too busy to get involved. Ian didn't push her, but she *would* be glad to see him again.

"Just won't be the same around here without you, Doc," said J.T.

"Well, let's not get sad. We've had a wonderful Thanksgiving meal thanks to the good Lord, who gives us all things freely, and to these beautiful ladies who worked hard to prepare it. Now, let's dive into those desserts. Look at that," he said, once again patting his round stomach. "I'm all swelled up."

"Me, too," Marv said. "I wonder what caused that?" Most everyone in the cozy dining room giggled.

"I want some of that pumpkin pie," Gwen spoke up. Elizabeth winced at her chiding.

"Everybody," Gracie announced proudly, "Elizabeth made the pumpkin pies."

"And they are beautiful," declared her Aunt Viney. "Grammy would be so proud."

Apple Muffin Cottage

"Let's *all* have pumpkin pie first," Gwen encouraged everyone with mocking, insincere congeniality as if she were trying to compliment Elizabeth, but Elizabeth and Victoria knew better.

"Elizabeth's pies are special," declared Dinky. "They have a special gredient just like Grammy's pies."

Elizabeth looked at Dinky, somewhat puzzled, wondering why he would say that.

"They are beautiful, Elizabeth," said sweet Victoria, wanting to encourage her cousin.

"Let's eat 'em then, instead of just lookin' at 'em," William scoffed.

"William Holley!" his mother scolded him to mind his manners.

Gracie cut and Viney served the pumpkin pie to each person on Grammy's best china dessert plates. They each took dollops of whipped cream from a lead crystal bowl as it was passed and heaped it onto their pie.

"Let's all wait and eat it together," Gwen prompted everyone, and they all agreed.

"Everybody have a slice?" Viney asked. "Okay, then

Thanksgiving at Apple Muffin Cottage

one, two, three—eat!" One by one, as everyone took a bite of Elizabeth's beautiful pumpkin pies, they gagged and spit it back out into their napkins—even Elizabeth.

"Way to go, Queenie!" Gwen cheered. "Way to go!"

William dared not laugh.

"Shut up, Gwen!" Michael yelled at his daughter.

Elizabeth was mortified. "Salt! Too much salt! How did that happen?" She shouted as tears ran down her face.

"I'm sorry, Elizabeth, I was only trying to help by puttin' in a seacrick gredient," cried Dinky. "I told Gwen that I'd put it in and was trying to help you." Everyone at the table glared at Gwen, knowing that she had set Elizabeth up for embarrassment.

"What do you mean, Davis Brent LeMaster? Did you touch my pies?"

"When Miss Patsy brought the bag of special gredients in, I put some in your pie filling," admitted Dinky. "I wanted your pies to be special like Grammy's with her seacrick gredient…"

"It was salt, you little twirp. Just salt!" Elizabeth practically screamed at her little brother. Tears spilled off of his little round cheeks, and his bottom lip quivered.

"Grammy always said she added *a cup of love* to everything she baked. *That* was her secret ingredient," Gracie said. "So, you see, Elizabeth, in his way, that's what Dinky *did* add to your pies, with his best intentions, I might add."

Elizabeth wouldn't look up. She sat with her head hung in shame, mortified over her culinary disaster but more ashamed that she yelled at her little brother and made him cry.

"It's okay, Dink, and I'm sorry I yelled at you," Elizabeth said quickly.

"Fanks, Elizabeth," Dinky answered, sniffing and wiping his nose on his shirt sleeve.

"I'm sure they would have been delicious, Elizabeth," Victoria tried to comfort her cousin.

"Thanks, Vic," Elizabeth sniffed. Gracie, Alice, and Viney were all wiping tears from their eyes.

"Who wants cake? I want some black walnut cake," beamed Gwen, glad about Elizabeth's calamity.

"I said shut up, Gwen," ordered her dad.

Lord, what do You do with rotten fruit?

Chapter 11:

Grammy's Gift

"In the house of the righteous there is much treasure..."

Proverbs 15:6 (NKJV)

December arrived unusually warm, with temperatures in the upper sixties. Gracie found it hard to think about Christmas shopping when the weather reminded her more of late spring with balmy breezes and blue skies. Even so, she knew it had to be done and forced herself to stick to her self-imposed "to-do" list and got ready to go to Brotherton. Her energy level was good today. She'd strike while the iron was hot and get at least the first shopping trip under her belt.

"I'm gonna help Uncle J.T. clean up his patch'ler pad," said Dinky on his way out the kitchen door earlier in the morning. He had a mop in one hand and a bucket in the other as Gracie helped him out.

"Go get 'em, tiger," Gracie said as she kissed him on

the head. "Be good and mind Uncle J.T." He assured her he would.

"See ya later, Mom," Elizabeth said, carrying a broom in one hand and a pan of slightly warm cinnamon rolls in the other.

"Love you. Behave yourselves." Gracie helped her daughter out the door. "And don't fight with your brother." She knew Elizabeth was still miffed at Dinky over the pumpkin pie fiasco at Thanksgiving. "Even though he is a little stinker," she added.

"I'll try. Love you, too. Bye, Mama," answered Elizabeth obligingly.

Gracie watched her children walk off the old back porch, down the three wooden steps onto a worn brick path leading to the kitchen garden. They continued along the outside edge of its fence onto a gravel walkway that led to J.T.'s door, where he was waiting for them to help him with his annual Christmas spruce-up.

He waved to Gracie.

"Make them mind," Gracie shouted to her brother as she waved back. J.T. nodded.

The old bunkhouse had been home to many fruit

pickers throughout the years during harvest times. J.T. laid claim to it in his late twenties. By then, it had been unused for a decade or more.

It was a one-room, long, narrow wooden structure, roughly 14x60, dotted along its length by a window here and there, a front door, and a back door.

Its furnishings included a sofa, a recliner, an entertainment center (complete with TV, DVD player, and stereo), a twin bed, a chest of drawers, a full-length mirror, and a computer desk and chair. In the middle of the expanse was a small table with two rocking chairs and a cast iron pot-bellied stove accompanied by a matching empty coal bucket. Baseboard heaters were added years ago to replace the inadequate heat source. There was also a small microwave and a dorm-sized refrigerator on a lone cabinet under one of the windows.

There was a bathhouse, too, complete with toilet, sink, and shower, built onto the back, whose only entry was from the outside—a major reason J.T. gave for disliking long, cold winters.

Armed with her checkbook, a cell phone, Elizabeth's wish list, and Dinky's letter to Santa, Gracie took advantage of J.T.'s need for once-a-year housecleaning help and headed for Brotherton, where she spent the better part of the morning in a "big box" store. She came home with a pirate ship and a sword that made clinking and clanging sounds for Dinky, along with some white long johns he could wear under his jeans when he went out to play in the snow. She bought a new comforter set for Elizabeth's bed, plus a few odds and ends and some groceries.

She was glad she'd made arrangements with J.T. to keep the kids until she called for them so she could get some rest and find a place to hide her Christmas "loot" away from their prying eyes. The best place would probably be the large closet in her room upstairs that used to be Grammy's.

Then she would have to fix something for lunch. She was certain the kids and J.T. would be hungry. After that, she'd check her email. Up until now, Maggie O'Riley had not responded to her request for an appraisal of her tea set. Gracie was growing more and more certain that it was not her mother at all, but she had a hard time getting it off her mind.

She felt a little anxious these days anyway. There was so much to be done before Christmas. The house needed to be cleaned from top to bottom before they could decorate.

Viney always had so much energy. Holleyhock Haven

Grammy's Gift

was decorated beautifully for the Christmas season (her house and the floral shop), and she'd even gotten Brotherton Arms' lobby and conference rooms done.

"I got the Arms finished today. It's gorgeous. Love for you to see it. I had an observer as I decorated the lobby. A beautiful older lady that lives there. She offered to hold some things for me until Amy came in. She didn't say much, but later, she brought Amy and me a couple of chai lattes from the coffee shop in the hotel. Sweet! I'd love to be that gracious someday." LaVinia rattled on in a call a few days after Thanksgiving.

"That's great, kiddo. I'm glad it went well for you. When I can, I'll stop in and look at it." Gracie hated to tell her she couldn't find a parking place today, but maybe next trip. She'd driven around the block several times and did enjoy seeing all of the outside Christmas decorations—the greenery and bows above the old town clock, the bells hanging from every old-fashioned street lamp, and all the store windows with flocked Christmas trees and lights.

It inspired her to "want to" make peanut butter fudge and listen to Christmas carols. She turned on Grammy's old radio that she always kept on the kitchen counter near the window and found a station playing a familiar rock'n'roll Christmas song.

It evoked a wonderful memory of Viney and herself "cutting a rug" with Grammy in the living room by the fireplace next to the old record player. Their Christmas tree stood in the opposite corner, decorated with shiny lights and bulbs, green and red paper chains, and red honeycomb bells. They giggled and danced, and each held one of Grammy's hands while their brothers colored Santa Claus in coloring books on the floor. They had her play the old forty-five record over and over again until their short-round Grammy got *tuckered out*. Then, Pop came in from town with oranges and Christmas candy. He said he'd seen one of Santa's elves peekin' round and that everybody should be real good—including Grammy.

Get up, Gracie! She admonished herself after her sweet daydream, half an hour's rest, and a cup of tea. *The day's a waistin'*. For some reason, she remembered her mother saying that very thing to her with a thick Irish accent when she was a little girl. Gracie smiled at the memory of that, too, as she took the packages up the stairs and into her bedroom.

The closet was exceptionally large and dark. She had been meaning for a while to replace its burned-out light bulb, but she needed a chair or ladder to stand on. Groping in the dark, Gracie pushed her way into the closet past her clothes, stepping on shoes on the floor as she went. This was a good hiding place because the kids would have trouble getting to the end of the closet if they went searching. *Not that they would.*

She continued to press and elbow her way to the back when suddenly her foot hit something unfamiliar under the lowest shelf. Gracie reached up high and sat her first package on the top shelf to free her hands before kneeling down on the floor to feel what she had stepped on. It was a large plastic box—something she and Viney had evidently missed when they put the last of Grammy's clothes away.

Gracie pulled it across the closet floor and set it out into the light of the bedroom, where she saw that Grammy had written *Gracie* on top of the red lid with a black permanent marker.

"Awww." Grammy had written her name. She had loved her grandmother more than anything else in the world until she had her children. Her brown eyes always twinkled with a light from within. She was cushy, sweet, warm, and a comfort to them all. Her years had been filled with life, love, wisdom, and Jesus, which she'd imparted to her grandchildren.

"What in the world?" Gracie said, astonished at the

find. She couldn't imagine how she had overlooked the box before.

Gracie examined it carefully. There appeared to be a quilting of some kind inside. She anxiously opened it with trembling hands. The box contained a beautiful unfinished quilt top, and laid on it were two stacks of letters and a picture.

Grammy had wrapped each bundle of letters in white notebook paper and tied them with a red ribbon. She had written *From Joshua* on the larger bundle. The small bundle, which contained only three letters, was marked *From Maggie*. Gracie gasped and put her hand to her heart.

She'd wondered whatever happened to any correspondence her dad had sent home. Grammy had tucked them away for safekeeping. She hastily read the first letter in Joshua's stack. Sadly, it was the last letter he wrote home to Maggie. She would read the rest of his letters another time.

A note Grammy pinned to the quilt read:

Maggie's quilt top she pieced for Gracie in '69. Quilt squares were cut out of scraps left over from Maggie and Gracie's Easter dresses that Maggie made in the spring of '69.

Grammy's Gift

Gracie was astonished, trying to take in the flood of heretofore unknown family history. After thirty-two years, she'd found a treasure that her mother's hands had made. Now, her fingers gently touched the quilt top, and she slowly lifted the picture of her mother and herself.

Oh, what a sweet face her mother had! She was beautiful! Gracie had forgotten just how beautiful. *They looked so happy together.* She turned the picture over and read her grandmother's familiar handwriting again:

*Maggie (pregnant with J.T.) and Gracie (age 4)
Easter 1969.*

She looked at their dresses in the picture and then looked at the quilt top. There, side by side, sewn together for over three decades, were pieces of their dress material—one square of pink and white sear-sucker, another square of green and white floral—alternated throughout the quilt.

It was all too much! Gracie laid the picture down, put her face in her hands, and sobbed uncontrollably. Years of sorrow and hurt seemed to melt away as she felt the love that her mother had pieced together.

"Oh, dear Lord," she cried, "my mother did love me. Thank You for revealing that to me, Lord. And thank you, Grammy, for this sweet gift."

Apple Muffin Cottage

Any bitterness or resentment that she ever had towards her mother disappeared in an instant. All she felt towards her now was love, forgiveness, and pity. She wanted so badly to put her arms around Maggie and tell her that she loved her. She wanted to let her know somehow that she held nothing against her. Something drastic must have happened for her to leave the children that she loved; Gracie understood that now.

As she picked up the letters, Gracie was still shocked to realize there had been correspondence from Maggie after her disappearance and wondered why Grammy never told her. She took a deep breath and composed herself, but still afraid of what she might read, she cautiously opened the first envelope marked *Grace*. The letter inside read:

August 14, 1969

Grace,

I'm going to find Joshua—I think he's in New York City, but first, I'm stopping at the hospital in Brotherton. I need some help. Please take good care of my babies. Tell them I'll be back. I promise.

Love,
Maggie

Grammy's Gift

Obviously, Maggie was beyond grief and not thinking clearly. She and Joshua had gotten married in New York City. In the last letter she received from him before he was killed, he said he'd take her back there someday. *Poor Mama! Bless her heart!* Gracie tenderly folded the letter and put it back in its envelope.

The next letter frightened her. It was postmarked July 1970, almost one year after Maggie had left. The return address was stamped *Brotherton*. After all these years of not knowing anything about her mother, now she was about to know. Her hands were shaking as she opened the second envelope and read the large childlike print that looked eerily like the handwriting inside the Regal Brookshire lid:

GRACE,

THE KIDS ARE YOURS. THEY DESERVE BETTER THAN ME.

MAGGIE

Gracie was convinced now that Maggie had a nervous breakdown after the death of her husband. She *had* loved her children in spite of what others had said. It was something beyond her control. She hadn't run away with a strange man, but she *was* trying to run to where she thought Joshua was. Grammy and Pop had known, too. That's why they never talked bad about Maggie but never tried to find her either.

The return address on the third envelope read *Timeless Treasures, Dublin, Ireland,* and was dated February 1975. That's how Grammy knew! And all the letter said was:

> BACK IN IRELAND LOOKING FOR MAGGIE
> SUE O'RILEY.

After this new revelation of Maggie, Gracie was more anxious than ever to get a reply to her email. Wiping her eyes, she put her discoveries back in the box, closed the lid, and hurried to the kitchen to turn on her laptop.

Click. Click.

You have 1 new message. Subject: tea set.

Mrs. LeMaster,

Could you please send me a picture of your tea set and the markings on the bottom so I may better assess it for you?

Maggie O

Gracie felt her heart beat faster. "Oh, Lord, please let this be my mother and help me to handle this the right way."

She positioned the upturned box lid partially behind the tea set on the kitchen table so that only the *Mag* in Maggie's name was visible in the first picture. If this was her mother, she would get the message. Hurriedly, she took the pictures that the mysterious Maggie O had requested and downloaded them into her computer, then attached copies to her email reply that read:

> *Attached you will find the pictures you have requested.*
>
> *Gracie LeMaster*

She was being bold, giving Maggie O her first name. Then, she also included her cell phone number, said another prayer, and hit the send button.

Now, she thought she could muster up the energy she needed to get ready for Christmas.

She had a feeling her mother was coming home.

Thank You, Lord! Thank You, Lord!

Chapter 12:

Going with J.T.

"In the day of my trouble I will call upon You, For You will answer me."

Psalm 86:7 (NKJV)

The weather changed drastically between the first and second weeks of December. Several inches of snow fell on Farmwell Valley, making it a little more challenging for J.T. to get a Christmas tree for Apple Muffin Cottage, but he was determined to try.

"Where's Uncle J.T.'s Chrissum Tree Farm?" Dinky seemed to think they were going clear to the North Pole to chop down a Christmas tree. He had never had a real one before, only artificial, already strung with lights. "Santa Claus gonna be there?"

Dinky's strawberry-blonde head turned to one side so quizzically, it made Gracie want to giggle. His sky-blue eyes and freckles, paired with his upturned nose, made him look elfish.

"Nope. Nope. I'm afraid Santa won't be there," Gracie answered, stifling a laugh.

"Uncle J.T.'s Christmas tree farm is on the slope of the South Ridge." She knew her four-year-old wouldn't fully understand, but she tried to explain anyway. "He started planting some of those trees years before you were born and some every year since."

"Are we gonna cut down all his Chrissum trees?"

"Nope. He's going to let you cut down the very first one this year, but before he can sell any of them, they have to be bigger."

"They reindeer on that farm?"

"Nope, no reindeer," Gracie answered.

"Who ever heard of a Chrissum tree farm with no reindeer?" Dinky puzzled.

"It's not really a farm," his mother replied, trying to make sure that his thumbs were both in the thumb holes of his mittens.

"Why's he call it a farm then if it ain't really a farm?" Dinky's question made sense to Gracie, but she got distracted by his use of bad grammar.

Going with J.T.

"Don't say 'ain't,' Dinky." Gracie pulled his toboggan down over his ears, made sure the zipper on his coat was pulled up under his chin, and turned him around towards the door. "Just go with Uncle J.T.," she said, giving him a slight nudge, "and have a good time. Try not to ask too many questions."

"Okie-dokie." In a flash, Dinky was out the door running through the yard, trying to kick up as much snow as he could with his superhero boots. About eight to ten inches of heavy, wet snow had fallen overnight.

Suddenly, Dinky stopped in mid-stride and fell backward into the fresh snow. He laid there for a few seconds, then started making jumping jack motions. He was fanning his arms upwards through the snow above his head and back down to his sides as his legs opened and closed like a pair of scissors.

"Oh, my gosh! Get up, Dinky, you'll be a mess," yelled his mother. "What next?" She mumbled to herself, shaking her head from side to side.

Dinky stood up, surveyed his masterpiece, and grinned. "Look, Mom," he said gleefully, pointing to the indention in the snow, "A angel. I made a snow angel."

Gracie couldn't be mad; he looked so proud. She smiled

at him and waved. He waved back, then turned around and ran to his uncle's big black truck.

"Hey, buddy," J.T. said as he dusted the snow off of Dinky's backside, then lifted him into the backseat of his four-wheel drive extended cab pickup.

"This things gots really big tires, Uncle J.T.," Dinky informed his uncle, who often used the truck for getting across the farm in places where there were no roads.

"Sure does," replied his uncle as he fastened Dinky's seatbelt.

"J.T., you be careful with my kids," Gracie yelled to her brother from the porch.

"I will. Don't worry. We're goin' by road today."

Most of the time, he would cut across Spirit Creek Farm in his truck and could be there in no time. Today, however, he would go by road since the snow was so deep and the kids were with him.

"Good," she answered. "I thought there was too much snow to go across the farm," she mumbled, knowing that J.T. probably couldn't hear her now.

"Where's Bethie? C'mon, Bethie, let's go!" J.T.

Going with J.T.

boomed so his niece could hear him.

He was anxious to show her and Dinky his trees, and he wanted to get there and back before dark because the temperature was supposed to plummet. *Even four-wheel drive vehicles don't do well on ice.* He was pleased, though, that the sky was clear and there was no more accumulation of snow expected today.

He would have to drive past Spirit Creek Farm and go south on Rt. 25, then turn onto the old logging road leading back to the south ridge. They would park at the top of the hill and walk the last quarter mile or so down the steep slope.

"Comin', Uncle J.T.," Elizabeth yelled as she ran out the door with a thermos of hot chocolate in one hand and a tote bag in the other. "I was getting our picnic lunch together," she explained.

Again, she was the perfect combination of youth and beauty. She wore a light blue parka, white gloves, and blue jeans tucked down into white boots. Her curly auburn hair hung loose from underneath a wide navy blue headband that covered her ears. Made redder by the cold, her rosebud lips and rosy cheeks made her eyes look even greener.

It was harder than usual for her to run. She felt bound up

from head to toe, and the snow was heavy, but she ran with a dramatic flair, pretending that she was in a commercial she'd seen one time for some peppermint gum.

With one upward movement, J.T. swept her up into the cab of his truck, too. "What kinda sandwiches?"

"Peanut butter and strawberry preserves. Six of them, just in case we get really hungry or stranded or something. And I brought some of my homemade Christmas ornament cookies, too."

"Sounds good." He hadn't taken time to eat breakfast, and he was already hungry. "Seat belts on?" J.T. sounded like an airplane pilot going through his checklist.

"Check," Elizabeth answered.

"Check," Dinky answered.

"Let's rock'n'roll," he said, always upbeat.

"Let's rock'n'roll," repeated Dinky, and he giggled with excitement that he could no longer contain when J.T. revved up the truck engine, put it in drive, and sent snow flying out from underneath the wheels as he spun out.

"Hold onto your hats, youngins," he said with great affect, "'cause we're gonna get us a Christmas tree."

Going with J.T.

"Yeah!" Dinky repeated with a growl. "We're gonna get us a Chrissum tree."

Gracie was standing at the door of Apple Muffin Cottage with her face in her hands. "Oh, dear Lord," she sighed, "please watch over my babies." She really *did* trust J.T. to be careful with her children, but she trusted the good Lord more.

"Hey, Uncle J.T.," Dinky piped up, "they reindeer on that Chrissum tree farm?"

"Well, ya never know whatcha might see on a Christmas tree farm," J.T. was trying to build up Dinky's excitement. He wanted him to always remember this day.

"We're going to find the most beautiful Christmas tree ever," Elizabeth said as she pictured in her mind how gorgeous it would look decorated and topped with their familiar china angel, the one she'd known all of her life. It had a satin cream-colored gown, painted-on blonde hair, tiny rosebud lips (like hers) painted red, miniature hands, and satin wings edged with lace. It wasn't Christmas until her mother took the angel out of her box on the top shelf in the hall closet of their old apartment.

Suddenly, Elizabeth recalled her dad holding her up to let her put the angel on top of their artificial tree. She must have only been about three or four. Her mother would never understand how much she missed her dad. Even though he was hardly ever home before he died, she longed to smell his aftershave again and feel his mustache tickle her cheek as he kissed her.

"Yeah, the most bee-u-tee-ful Chrissum tree ever," parroted Dinky from his booster seat in the back. He was fascinated by the way the wipers would smack away the big chunks of snow that blew up off of the hood onto the windshield every now and then. His head rocked back and forth in time to them and to the tune of J.T. singing.

Jingle bells, jingle bells, jingle all the way...

The truck cab was filled with the happy song as they made their way over the snow-covered road past their farm. When they turned onto Rt. 25, much to their surprise, they noticed that the snow plow had been there before them, and the road was clear.

"Too bad Victoria and William are Christmas shopping today," said J.T. "Oh, well, I'll take them out sometime this week."

"Yeah, too bad," said Elizabeth half-heartedly. She really was secretly glad that her cousins were out of town today. She didn't want to have to share Uncle J.T. with

Going with J.T.

them or have to deal with William.

Although, Rt. 25 had been cleared, when J.T. turned onto the old logging road the snow was very deep. "The snow plow sure hasn't been up here," he remarked.

"No, sir-ree!" Dinky exclaimed as he peered out the windows and saw the snow-covered road.

"Look!" Elizabeth yelled. "There's Miss Patsy's car on the side of the road. I think she's stuck."

"I think you're right. That is Miss Patsy." J.T. slowly pulled his truck in behind her. "I'll see if I can help. You guys stay put," he insisted.

"Hey, girl, what's going on?" J.T. yelled as he knocked on her driver's side window.

"Oh, J.T., thank God!" Miss Patsy said as she rolled down her window. "You're a prayer answered. I started to slide and got over in this ditch. I am really stuck."

"Looks like it," he said as he surveyed the snow packed under her vehicle. "What in the world are you doing out here?"

"Well, Mr. Tabor, who lives on top of that hill over there..." she said, pointing to a tiny little house where smoke was curling up out of its chimney.

"Yeah, I know Mr. Tabor," J.T. informed her. He had known him as long as he could remember. Mr. Tabor lived in the last house along the old logging road. "I used to come visit him with Pop when I was younger." Mr. Tabor and Pop used to chew tobacco and spit into the fire, which made a sizzling, hissing sort of noise that J.T. still remembered.

"Well, he's feeble and can't get into town to get his groceries anymore, so I've been delivering to him. I knew he would need some things. I should have called him and gotten out here yesterday." Miss Patsy shook her head in disgust, mad at herself. "Now I'm stuck, and he still doesn't have what he needs."

"We can take care of both," J.T. said, reassuring Miss Patsy. "Come on. Hop in my truck, and I'll get his stuff. We'll have his groceries to him in no time. Then, I'll come back and haul you out of here. I've got a tow chain in the back."

"Really? You don't mind? Mom hates me coming out here. I hated to have to call her and tell her I was stuck."

"Really. I don't mind," J.T. said with a broad smile. He was glad for the opportunity to spend time with her. She was the most beautiful woman he had ever seen. Miss

Going with J.T.

Patsy's blue eyes sparkled, and her long, curly blonde hair parted on the side framed her face with cascades of spirals.

"Okay, Sir Galahad, let's do it! Everything's in the trunk," Miss Patsy grinned back at him and looked straight into his eyes. She gathered her purse and gloves from the front seat and got out of her small car, then handed her keys to J.T. He noticed how nice she looked with her jeans tucked down into her leather boots. In her winter-white jacket with pink faux fur around the hood, he thought she looked like an angel.

"Hey, Bethie, scoot yourself over so Miss Patsy can get in the front seat there with you," J.T. said with excitement in his voice that he couldn't seem to contain.

"Hey, Miss Patsy!" Elizabeth greeted her friend with great enthusiasm.

"Hey, guys. How are you?" Patsy called out as J.T. gave her a hand up into the truck cab. Then, he went back to get Mr. Tabor's groceries. There were several bags and some smaller boxes packed into one big box, along with a large container of soup. He put it all in the bed of his truck.

"Hey, Miss Patsy," Dinky called out, "we're goin' to a Chrissum tree farm to find a reindeer." His voice squeaked when he talked.

"You are?"

"We might even see Santa Claus there, and then we're gonna get us a bee-u-tee-ful Chrissum tree. And drink hot chocolate."

"Wow, does that ever sound fun!" Miss Patsy exclaimed.

"Come go wif us, Miss Patsy!" Dinky excitedly extended the invitation.

"Yeah, please come and go with us," Elizabeth chimed in. "It would be so much fun."

"Oh, I couldn't, sweetie. I've got to get these groceries to Mr. Tabor and then get out of that snow bank," she said apologetically as J.T. got in the driver's seat. "I hope I'm not interfering with your plans, J.T."

"Not at all, especially if you go on up the road with us." He looked sheepishly at her and continued with the invitation, "I'll have you back here, outta that snow bank, and home before dark." He was quiet for a moment while she was thinking. "Come and see my Christmas trees with us," he implored. "Got any more deliveries after this?"

"Nope," she said, thinking she'd just received a very sweet invitation.

Going with J.T.

"Do you have to work in the store today?" asked J.T. further.

"Nope. Not today."

"Any voice students?"

"Never on Saturday," she answered smiling, knowing that she had no more excuses left except trying to explain to her mom that she would be with J.T. Barton. Ever since Miss Patsy and J.T. were kids together in school, her mother had practically despised him and wanted her to have nothing to do with him. "But he's a good guy," Patsy always argued with her mom.

"I don't care! I don't want you seeing him again. You could have any other boy in school." But BevAnn was the one that didn't understand. Patsy never wanted any other boy.

"Hey, Harper. Hi, Patsy here. Listen, tell my mom I'm going to be out for a while and I'll be home by dark. Okay, thanks, Harper. Bye." Miss Patsy closed her cell phone and grinned at J.T. "I'll let the stock boy tell her," Miss Patsy pronounced, then she giggled.

"Okay then," J.T. looked at her with hesitation in his eyes. "Are you sure?"

"I'm sure."

Apple Muffin Cottage

"Then let's rock'n'roll," J.T. said laughingly.

"Yeah, let's rock'n'roll," yelled Dinky clapping his hands.

"Alright." Miss Patsy agreed. "Let's rock'n'roll." Then she started to sing:

Jingle bells, jingle bells, jingle all the way...

J.T., Elizabeth, and Dinky all joined in as they traveled happily toward Mr. Tabor's little house.

Chapter 13:

Trees

"...He said, 'It is more blessed to give than to receive.'"

Acts 20:35 (NKJV)

Elizabeth couldn't contain her joy. She giggled and laughed, and so did Dinky. They thought it was wonderful having Miss Patsy and Uncle J.T. together and all of them having fun.

The snow got deeper the further they drove on the logging road. J.T. didn't let on, but he was concerned. He hadn't counted on such big snow drifts. The kids would be disappointed if they had to turn back. He would make a decision after they got the groceries delivered. Once they were on the hill, he could see further up the road and better assess the situation.

J.T. gunned his pickup and drove right to Mr. Tabor's house without a problem. The old fellow heard the truck engine and walked, with his cane, to the front door to see who in the world had made it up *his* hill in spite of all the snow.

"Well, 'pon my honor," he exclaimed with a toothless grin as he stepped outside, "thought I's gonna have to go without my coffee a day or two."

"Not if we could help it, Mr. Tabor," J.T. answered as he got out of the truck. He stepped up on the running board, reached over into the truck bed, and handed Miss Patsy some things to carry in. He'd get the rest.

"Well, come in, come in," Mr. Tabor motioned with one hand, "and bring them youngins too." He always loved children and could see Elizabeth and Dinky as he peered down through the windshield.

"Let's all go in for a while, guys," J. T. instructed. "And Bethie, bring that picnic bag." Elizabeth and Dinky followed J.T. and Miss Patsy into the old man's house.

J.T. continued on into the kitchen and sat Miss Patsy's delivery on the table before returning to the living room.

"Mr. Tabor, this is my niece Bethie and my nephew Davis."

"Hello. Welcome. Welcome. Nice to meet ya. Take your coats off, youngins, and set down a bit."

"Glad to see you, Mr. Tabor." Patsy leaned over and gave the little old man a hug.

The small house was surprisingly charming, extremely warm, and clean. An old sofa sat against the longest wall, directly across from the roaring fireplace. It was covered with a large handmade wedding ring quilt.

A double bed with a huge mahogany headboard in the only bedroom of the house was visible from the living room. It, too, was made up neatly with a quilt handmade by the late Mrs. Tabor. She had won several awards for her creations and had taught Grace Barton many things.

There were no other bedrooms in the house. The Tabors had built their house by hand and decided to add a bedroom each time they had a child. Sorrowfully, there had been two miscarriages and a stillbirth. They never had the need for another bedroom.

A rocking chair in the middle of the room faced a small TV, which was perched atop a wooden table under the front window. Old sepia-colored photographs of people from long ago in heavy oval frames hung on the walls around the room. There were women with high collars and hair piled high on their heads and men with handlebar mustaches and slicked-down hair with middle parts.

More recent photographs that were in color but still looked old sat around the room on side tables and the mantel.

"Mr. Tabor, how are you, sir? I've been meaning to come visit you for the longest time." J.T. was apologetic. Mr. Tabor and his late wife were good friends with Pop and Grammy for years. Many times, he sat quietly and listened while they all visited and shared stories about growing up together.

"Well, sometimes I feel pretty bad. But the good Lord's seen fit to leave me here for a while longer, so I try not to complain. Glad to have some company today."

"We sure are glad to visit ya," J.T. said happily.

"I brought your pain reliever, too, Mr. Tabor," said Miss Patsy loudly so he could hear.

"Oh, thank you, darlin'. You're a good girl." He reached over and patted her arm. She smiled at him sweetly, feeling an almost familial connection to him.

"So nice when Patsy comes to visit," he said, smiling at her.

While the grownups talked, Elizabeth and Dinky looked around the room.

"Oh my Gosh! Dinky, look!" Elizabeth whispered, astonished as she picked up a double picture frame off the end table. On one side, there was a print of an old hippie standing by a Corvette and a picture of a young girl that looked like Miss Patsy on the other side. The young man had a wide mustache, long bushy hair, and he wore a leather vest with no shirt underneath.

"It's that heeven and Miss Patsy!" Dinky whispered back.

"I know. Couldn't be the same one. Could it? And that couldn't be Miss Patsy. This picture is older than she is." Elizabeth was puzzled.

Dinky shrugged his small shoulders and started for Mr. Tabor's cat.

"I'm gonna put us on some coffee if you don't mind. Then, I'm going to fix you some lunch. I brought you some soup," Miss Patsy said on her way to the kitchen where J.T. had set the box on the small table.

"She takes good care of me," the old man said, beaming. "She's a good Christian woman. Reminds me of my sister Kate—somethin' about her does. "

"She's one in a million," J.T. said, then he pointed to

the sofa for the kids to sit down. "Won't ya stay and have some soup with me?"

"Well, Mr. Tabor, I believe we will," J.T. answered quickly. He knew Pop's friend was all alone in the world and would enjoy some company. "As a matter of fact, I think we have some sandwiches to throw in with that soup."

"Oh, boy," said the old man, happy that his invitation had been accepted, "and don't that coffee smell good?" Miss Patsy had just opened the can in the next room. "Coffee always smells better than it tastes. Don't ya think?"

"Yes, sir, but most of the time, it sure does taste good, too," J.T. replied as he took off his coat and hat.

"I know it, I know it," Mr. Tabor repeated while grinning and shaking his head. His eyes twinkled merrily.

Miss Patsy could hear their conversation from the kitchen while she heated up the vegetable soup. She knew J.T. was trying to make a lonely old man feel not so lonely today. They were reminiscing now about Mr. and Mrs. Barton. She felt privileged to hear their memories.

"Elizabeth, would you like to come in and help me set the table?" Miss Patsy knew her little friend must feel out of place in the living room with the men. Mr. Tabor's big gray cat, Smokey, was keeping Dinky busy on the sofa.

"Sure, Miss Patsy."

"So, you've got some sandwiches in that tote bag you want to share?"

Elizabeth took six sandwich bags out of the tote and laid them on the table.

"Yes, and I have some Christmas cookies, too."

"Oh, great. How perfect! We'll have a little Christmas party. Look! Look at what I brought Mr. Tabor." Her eyes sparkled as she pulled a narrow box out of one of the bags.

"It's a little fiber optic Christmas tree. It has lots of different colored lights that twinkle. Do you think he'll like it? And look, I bought some little ornaments for it and a small star for the top."

"We'll set it right in the middle of the table, so he can't miss it when he walks in." Miss Patsy was very happy to do something special for her elderly friend.

The diminutive tree came out of the box easily with its own small stand. Both pieces, once put together, stood about eighteen inches tall. She flipped the switch, and colored lights started to brighten, then dim, then brighten again. Red, blue, green, and yellow lights came on and went off intermittently.

"Ooh, how pretty," Elizabeth sighed.

"Look in these bags, Bethie." Miss Patsy had never called her that before. Only Uncle J.T. and her mom called her Bethie, but she didn't mind. "I've brought him Christmas candy and tangerines. I just wanted to do something special for him, ya know?" She had already put away his bread, ground meat, raisin bran, milk, bacon, and eggs.

"I know," Elizabeth acknowledged. She thought her friend had a heart of gold, and she seemed to love everybody and everything, unlike her mother, BevAnn.

"Elizabeth, here are two pretty plates to put your sandwiches and cookies on. Oh, those look so good."

"Gee, Miss Patsy," Elizabeth exclaimed as she stood back and looked at the table, "that really looks nice and Christmas-y."

"Well, let's get them in here and get this show on the road then," Miss Patsy smiled.

"Smellin' good in there," J.T. yelled.

"Then come and get it!" Miss Patsy was anxious to see the look on Mr. Tabor's face when he spied the little tree.

"Well, 'pon my honor," he exclaimed as he shuffled slowly through the kitchen door. "Ain't that purty?"

"Here, everybody's got to put a little decoration or two on it before we eat. And Mr. Tabor, you put the star on top," Miss Patsy directed.

"Well, ain't that somethin'," said the old fellow as he grinned and shook his head in disbelief that he would ever have a Christmas tree again. "And look at them cookies. Don't they look good!"

Elizabeth smiled.

"Just one problem," said J.T. "We're short a chair for the table."

"Grab a plastic one off the back porch there, son," Mr. Tabor instructed him as he put the miniature silver star on the top of the twinkling tree.

J.T. stepped outside to get a chair. He walked over to the left side of the old man's porch, where he could see the upper end of the logging road, which was covered with snow drifts three and four feet high. He knew he couldn't run the risk of getting stuck in those. As bad as he hated to, he was going to have to tell the kids they couldn't go any further today.

But, surprisingly, there was an astounding view of Spirit Creek Farm's south ridge slope from this vantage point. From where he was standing, he could see practically every acre of his tree farm below. He spent a few seconds looking at it before he shivered, grabbed the chair, and went back into the kitchen.

"Pop would have been proud of my tree farm down there, Mr. Tabor," J.T. said as he sat the chair down beside Miss Patsy. Dinky and Elizabeth were putting the last of the ornaments on the tree.

"Oh, he was, son, he was. Proud of your Christmas trees and your fruit trees," Mr. Tabor answered. "Bragged on ya all the time. Said 'that J.T. really knows his trees.'"

J.T. beamed with pride, scratched his head, and smiled at Miss Patsy. She thought she saw his eyes mist over a bit.

"Mr. Tabor, I'm sure you want to say grace," Miss Patsy prompted her friend.

"Well, let's all hold hands and say it together," he insisted.

"God is great. God is good. And we thank Him for our food.

By His hands, we are fed. Give us, Lord, our daily bread.

Amen."

"Amen, dig in," Dinky added.

"Mr. Tabor," J.T. said after lunch, "I wish you'd tell the kids and Miss Patsy here about the time your brother-in-law Bernie and his dad got that Model T back in the thirties." J.T. knew Mr. Tabor loved telling stories about the *good old days*.

"Well, youngins," said Mr. Tabor, not needing to be asked twice, "my brother-in-law Bernie, me and him was kids together; he married my sister Kate. Well, his pa, old man Andrews, was a real wheeler-dealer. One day he took ta wantin' a automobile 'cause everybody else up along the crick where they lived had 'em for years, but he never had one hisself. Road a horse everywhere he went. This was back in, oh, about 1935.

"He told his boy Bernie ta come go with him they was goin' in ta Hope Springs ta git a car. He knowed a old fellar that was gonna give 'em a right smart deal on one, and maybe Bernie could use it ta start peddlin' eggs (they raised chickens) and make him a little extry cash.

"So they walked in ta town and looked over an old black 1922 Model T Ford that old feller had. It didn't have no windows, of course, none of 'em did that was that old. And it didn't have no top 'cept an old collapsible leather roof ya pulled up and over and attached ta the windshield or folded it back out of the way. But there was just one problem. That old car didn't have a windshield. One was supposed ta set right straight up and down on top of the hood of that old car like a winda frame, but all the glass had been busted out, so the old feller that owned it just took the whole thing off. So that old car was open all the way 'round just like a old row boat.

"Now, Bernie's pa walked around it and kicked the little skinny tires to make sure all the spokes was in the wheels. He looked it over real good like he know'd what he was a lookin' at. Then, he asked the old man how much he wanted fer it. The old man thinks fer a minute and then says in a funny high-pitched voice, 'Since it don't have no windshield, just give me ten dollars, that's all I got in 'er.'

"'I'll take 'er,' says old man Andrews, who thought he was makin' a right smart deal. But they was another problem. He didn't know how ta drive. So, he say's ta Bernie, 'Boy you're gonna have ta drive this derned thing home.'

"Well, Bernie'd never drove a car before neither, he was only twelve, but told his pa *okay he'd give it a try*. So, in hops old man Andrews in the front seat, and in hops Bernie behind the wheel (after he cranks 'er up) puts it in gear, and down the road they go.

"Now, the further they'd go, the more comfortable Bernie gets and starts ta feelin' real proud that he's drivin' and picks up his speed til—heck, they go like he's been drivin' all his life.

"He was makin' a purty good clip when all of a sudden he saw the crick crossin'. He forgot they'd have ta drive through the crick on the way home. But he wudn't sure he knew how to drive through that water, although it wudn't none too deep. Well, Bernie got skeert and panicked. He grabbed hard on ta that steerin' wheel til his knuckles was white and hit those brakes so hard he practically stood that old car right on its nose.

"I asked him when he was tellin' me about it, I said, 'Bernie, then what happened?'

'What happened? I'll tell you what happened. Pa bounced up out a that seat and shot straight across the hood a that car like a frog and landed right in the middle of the crick.'"

Apple Muffin Cottage

"Oh, no," shouted Miss Patsy, "did it kill him?"

"No," said Mr. Tabor. "Old man Andrews just got up and shook hisself off, climbed back in that old car wet, and said, 'Boy, let's try that agin'. So, Bernie drove on right across that crick, and right on home they went."

"And he went into the creek like a frog," cackled Dinky along with everyone else at the table.

"And you know, 'pon my honor, that old Bernie peddled eggs for years out a that old car. Made enough money to put hisself through barber college. Moved to North Carolina and made a real good livin'."

Everyone laughed even harder now.

"Oh, that's too funny," Elizabeth giggled, "and Bernie was only twelve."

"I'd say Pa made a pretty good investment," Miss Patsy declared, laughing and holding her stomach. This was the best day she could remember having in all her life. She'd never been so happy.

"He *was* a real wheeler-dealer," J.T. said, slapping his knee and laughing so hard he wheezed.

"Pop always loved that story, Mr. Tabor."

Trees

Mr. Tabor was grinning a wide toothless grin. His eyes were sparkling. He loved to make people laugh.

"Yeah, the funny thing—there Bernie was a barber, and his boy wouldn't let him cut his hair. He ended up bein' one of them famous rock'n'roll singers. Had hair clear down his back. Pete Andrews is his name. He used ta live in New York City, but he works outa Raleigh, North Carolina, now. He's called me every week for the last thirty years. He's a good boy."

"Oh, I remember him," Patsy exclaimed with excitement. "He was really good. I still hear his songs on the oldies station every now and then. I didn't know he was your nephew. How exciting."

"Used ta come stay with us some in the summers back years ago. Last time he stayed was summer of '69. He'd got back from Vietnam in '68, my sister Kate passed away, and he was real restless for a while. Had a lot to get off his mind, I suppose. He had a wife he was separated from, but he decided to go back to New York and try to make it work out, and it did. They were married for several years until she died of a really bad disease. Then, he took care of Bernie til he died back in ninety-eight." Mr. Tabor looked lost in thought as he talked about his nephew. "He's like a son to me. He's a real good boy, always taking care of somebody else."

Apple Muffin Cottage

"He slips in to see me every now and then. Keeps wanting me to move down south with him. Never wanted to leave home, but I think I'm gonna have to by next spring. Too old to stay alone anymore."

"Sounds like a nice guy. We will miss you, Mr. Tabor, but you have to do what you have to do," J.T. stated. He wondered why he'd never seen or heard of Pete Andrews before now.

"Was that him in the picture standing by that car, Mr. Tabor?" Elizabeth's curiosity was making her bold.

"Yep, little missy. That's him. Just looked like an old hippie, didn't he?" Mr. Tabor laughed. "He's worth several million dollars, but you'd never know it."

"Can I see?" Miss Patsy got up and went to the living room to see Mr. Tabor's famous nephew. Everybody followed her.

"I've never seen this picture before," Patsy said as she looked closely at the young man in the picture. He looked so familiar. *An old hippie... an old hippie...* Something about that resonated through her mind. She'd heard it somewhere before.

"I just put it out there. Found it in a box yonder under

the bed when I was lookin' fer my house slippers. Been under there fer years."

Elizabeth brought everyone's attention to the young girl in the attached photo.

"Oh, look, Miss Patsy! It's you. How old were you when this was taken?

"Bethie, that's not me."

"That's my sister Kate when she was just a girl." Mr. Tabor had noticed the resemblance, too. "I told you that you reminded me of her."

"Yeah, I do kind of look like her." Miss Patsy was puzzled because there was more than just a slight resemblance.

After lunch, she and Elizabeth cleaned up the kitchen. Then Dinky helped Mr. Tabor put his Christmas candy and tangerines in a box that he kept under his bed. Mr. Tabor insisted that Dinky and Elizabeth take *a handful.*

J.T. was sitting in the rocking chair that he'd turned towards the fire and was watching the glowing orange and red coals. He hated to disappoint the kids and Miss Patsy, but he couldn't put off telling them any longer that the road was impassable.

"Well," J.T. said as he cleared his throat, "I'm afraid the snow's too piled up on the road to continue on to the tree farm."

"Oh, no, Uncle J.T., we can't see your Chrissum tree farm?" Dinky asked, somewhat devastated, sitting on the living room floor petting the cat. His face was getting red, and he was trying not to cry.

J.T. didn't know what else to say. He kept staring into the fireplace.

"But how will we get us a Chrissum tree?" Dinky wanted to know. "And I was wantin' to see a reindeer."

"Well, little feller, I can't do nothin' 'bout that reindeer, but I can show ya where there's some mighty purty little Christmas trees just waitin' to be cut down, taken home, and decorated." Mr. Tabor grinned at Dinky and patted him on the head. Dinky smiled back at him with renewed hope.

That got J.T.'s attention, and he stood up out of the rocking chair. "Really, where's that, Mr. Tabor?"

"Just off the right side of m'back porch and up the hill a little ways. I set some Douglas firs out a few years ago ta keep my hillside from slippin'. It'd tickle me to death if ya'd get one of 'em."

"Kids, get your coats on—we're gettin' us a Christmas tree today, after all," J.T. beamed with joy. "Let's rock'n'roll!"

"Yeah, let's rock'n'roll," mimicked Dinky.

"They's an axe laying on the porch near the washin' machine."

Mr. Tabor grabbed his cane from off the kitchen chair and a jacket from a hook on the wall beside the back door and tagged along with J.T., Miss Patsy, Elizabeth, and Dinky as they filed happily out the door one by one.

"C'mere a minute," J.T. said as he walked towards the left side of the porch, "I want to show you guys something. Look down there. That's my tree farm." He smiled with pride.

"Wow, look how straight all those rows are, Uncle J.T.," Elizabeth exclaimed.

"What a beautiful view of it from up here," said Miss Patsy. She was amazed at how much they could see. There were perfectly straight rows of partially snow-covered evergreens grouped by height, laid out below like straight stitches across a quilt. She was so proud of J.T., too. He had put a lot of years and hard work into this venture.

"Dink, look, Dink! There goes your reindeer!" J.T. was stunned to spy a large buck with a huge rack of antlers among his trees down below.

"Wow, a reindeer," exclaimed Dinky with unbridled excitement, "on a real Chrissum tree farm!"

"Yeah, imagine that," J.T. said with relief. He was so glad the kids and Miss Patsy weren't disappointed. Patsy smiled at him. *What a perfect day!*

"Come back and visit again real soon," yelled Mr. Tabor, waving from the front porch as he looked down on J.T.'s big black truck with the nice fir tree thrown into the bed. They had cut down the prettiest one at Mr. Tabor's insistence.

Earlier, as Dinky and J.T. climbed the back hill to get to it, Dinky had asked, "Is this the way to heaven, Uncle J.T.?" because they were going up so high. J.T. said he wished it was that easy and laughed a little.

"'Cause of Jesus dying on that ole cross for our sins, and coming back to life agin, it ain't hard at all. That's what Mama and Miss Patsy tell me." Dinky never looked up but kept climbing.

"Yeah, that's what I hear," J.T. answered him thoughtfully.

"What a wonderful afternoon," Miss Patsy said joyfully as they turned back onto the old logging road.

"I am so glad we got to bless Mr. Tabor today." Elizabeth was somewhat smug.

"I think he was the one that blessed us, Elizabeth. He gave us the best Chrissum tree ever."

"He sure did," said J.T.

"Yes, he certainly did." Miss Patsy wiped a tear from her eye, thinking about how much she loved Mr. Tabor. He was such a dear friend to her. She thought of him as family.

"Yep, Dinky, I guess you're right. He sure did," Elizabeth agreed. "But, wait, we didn't get to drink our hot chocolate!"

"Well, let's have some when we get Miss Patsy's car out of that ditch," her uncle replied as he drove back through the tracks in the snow his truck made earlier.

Anything to keep her with us longer. J.T. smiled.

Miss Patsy smiled at him sweetly as she sang with Elizabeth.

Apple Muffin Cottage

Deck the halls with boughs of holly,

Fa la la la la la la la la!

Chapter 14:

A Night for Miracles

"...behold the Lamb of God, which taketh away the sin of the world."

John 1:29 (KJV)

"Mom, where's my halo? Have you seen my halo?" Elizabeth yelled down through the vent in her bedroom floor to her mom in the kitchen.

Gracie stopped in mid-stride on her way through to the dining room and yelled back at her anxious preteen daughter, "Check the table by the front door. It's right where you left it."

"Thanks!" Elizabeth shouted back.

"You're welcome."

As an afterthought, Gracie paused in the kitchen long

enough to stir the meatballs in the slow cooker. The ham was cooked and being kept warm underneath a tent of aluminum foil on top of the old wood-burning stove. She had a cheese ball in the refrigerator along with a vegetable tray. There were breads and crackers, Christmas cookies and candy in decorated trays and tins, and a red velvet cake on a clear glass cake stand sitting on the dining room table beside the empty punch bowl. Everything was ready for their family Christmas Eve party after the play. J.T. and the Holleys would join her and the kids for a little while, and then tomorrow, they would all gather at Holleyhock Haven for Christmas dinner.

"Dinky!" Gracie yelled. "Are you ready? We have to be at the church in half an hour. Come on, let's go."

Between making sure costumes were ready, wrapping last-minute gifts, and cooking, she had managed to check her emails and was pleased to find one from the mysterious Maggie O, which read:

> *May I ask where and when you acquired your tea set? Maggie O*

Gracie was happy that Maggie had taken the bait. Her return email read:

> *It was my mother's from Ireland.*

A Night for Miracles

She'd have to give it further attention after Christmas.

"I don't wanna be a wise man. I just want to be an old shepherd or somethin'." Dinky said as he met her in the living room beside the beautifully decorated Christmas tree from Mr. Tabor's hill. He had a gold cardboard crown on top of his head and a striped bathrobe tied around his waist with a braided gold cord.

"But, what a handsome little wise man you are," said Gracie, complimenting him with a smile.

"I'm skeerd. I don't wanna say, 'I brought some gold for the Christ child' in front a all those people."

"It will be okay, son. Just do your best. Miss Patsy is counting on you."

"Yeah, and Uncle J.T.'s gonna give me five dollars," Dinky smiled, remembering a bribe from his uncle.

"Make sure Uncle J.T. gets his money's worth then," said Gracie, still encouraging her four-year-old as they walked to her car through the cold, crunchy snow in front of Apple Muffin Cottage. It was already dark by 5:30 when they left the house, and the icicle lights hanging off the edge of the roof weren't on yet because J.T. had set the timer switch for 6:00. The house and yard both were completely dark except for the light of the Christmas tree glowing from the living room window.

"What a clear night," Gracie said as she looked up with wonder into the star-filled sky. "Look at all those stars."

"There must be a million of 'em," Dinky replied, looking up as he walked.

"The moon's pretty bright, too," added Elizabeth. Even with her halo and cardboard wings in hand, she still managed to point toward the horizon.

"What a perfect night for Santa Claus to visit us from the North Pole," Gracie said, taking the opportunity to add a little drama and excitement to the evening.

Dinky stood very still and looked upward, craning his neck until the cardboard crown slid to the very back of his head.

"I wonder what the sky looked like the night baby Jesus was born in Bethlehem?" he asked, almost enraptured by the sight up above him.

"There was one big bright star that shone down on the stable where he lay," said Gracie, "and the sky was full of angels saying…"

A Night for Miracles

"Glory to God in the highest and on earth, peace, good will toward men," Elizabeth added, finishing her mom's sentence because that was her line in the Christmas play.

Gracie smiled and made a conscious decision to register this once-in-a-lifetime moment in her memory. She hoped Elizabeth and Dinky would remember it always.

"We'd better hurry, or we'll be late," Gracie said, but reluctant to give up this moment.

When they arrived at Hope Springs Church, it was all lit up from within. Two black lamp posts that sat on either side of the steps leading up to the churchyard from the street were coiled roundabout with red velvet ribbon. A brilliant light shone from their lanterns and lit the stone pathway leading to the little white church nestled in snow. Two huge evergreen wreaths, accented with large red bows, adorned the heavy oak doors where streams of yellowish light escaped from underneath.

"Wow!" said Gracie as she walked towards the church with Elizabeth and Dinky. "What a beautiful sight. I forgot how pretty this old church is at Christmastime."

Every illuminated stained-glass window down both sides of the building was emitting a blue, red, and purple glow, and even the bell tower in the tall spire was crowning the church with a heavenly radiance. It was breathtaking!

"It looks like a Christmas card," someone said as they passed Gracie, and she agreed with them wholeheartedly.

The beauty and peacefulness of this old church in the new-fallen snow reminded her that through the years, many had prayed here, felt conviction of sin, renewed their faith here, and worshipped here. Lives had been changed here. It was God's house, and the reverence she felt seemed to fill her with joy and wonder. She knew all things were possible with God, and He could do exceedingly abundantly above all she could ask or think. So, Gracie truly believed that tonight was a night for miracles.

Elizabeth and Dinky made their way to the back of the church, where Miss Patsy (the Christmas play author and director) and the other children were all waiting for them. Gracie sat at the end of a pew near the front of the church where she could take pictures. Several others in the congregation came by, shook her hand, and said hello.

Miss Patsy's mom, BevAnn, walked into the front of the church from a side door and stepped up to the piano to arrange her sheet music. No one would ever guess her real age. She was very petite with black hair and sapphire-blue eyes. Her makeup was flawless, and her red suit, white blouse, and red high heels were a perfect ensemble. She was beautiful! Gracie smiled, acknowledging a glance from her, but she never smiled back. *Definitely rotten fruit.*

"This seat taken?" A masculine voice interrupted Gracie's thoughts.

"It is now, little brother," Gracie replied to J.T. as he sat down. She noticed that the pews were filling up quickly on the other side of the room.

"Thanks." He smiled, and once again, Gracie thought he was so very handsome. She was anxious for Patsy to see him all dressed up in his red turtle neck sweater and black leather jacket.

Miss Patsy stepped out from a side door, walked to the microphone, and tapped it.

"Testing. One. Two." The sound reverberated throughout the church.

"Testing. One. Two," she repeated. Then she nodded to someone in the back of the church and cleared her throat.

"We here at Hope Springs Church would like to welcome you to our 75th annual Christmas pageant." She saw J.T. and smiled at him very sweetly and blushed. He grinned lovingly at her.

"Tonight," she continued, "our children are presenting a play entitled *The First Christmas*. We hope you will be blessed by it. Now, I would like to introduce to you Reverend Alejandro Rodriguez, our interim pastor."

A dark-haired, dark-skinned young man stepped up to the microphone and said with a thick Spanish accent, "Good evening."

He had a very broad smile and beautiful white teeth.

"Merry Christmas! Or, like we say where I come from in South America, *Feliz Navidad!*"

"*Feliz Navidad*," replied the congregation in unison.

"I'm glad to be with you at Hope Springs Church for a little while until your new pastor arrives in a few months. While I'm here, I hope we can get to know each other and serve together for the uplifting of the Lord's kingdom. And please, just call me Pastor Al. It will make things easier for everybody. So, let us pray," he said, bowing his head. "Father in heaven, in the name of Your Son and our Savior Jesus Christ, bless this night and reveal its true meaning to us through this performance. Let each one of us know that it is truly a night for miracles and that only You can make them happen. Now, Father, may hearts and minds be renewed for Your glory. Amen."

A Night for Miracles

"There it is again," said Gracie to herself, "a night for miracles."

Someone in the back of the church dimmed the lights. Harper Randal, the teenage stock boy from BevAnn's grocery store, pulled back curtains across a rope, revealing a makeshift stage in front of the choir loft, lit from above by a single spotlight. Victoria was Mother Mary kneeling beside a manger, and a short Joseph was standing by her side.

Scattered on the stage beside the manger among bails of straw were several young children dressed like shepherds in bathrobes and sandals with staffs in their hands. Next to them were the tiny children from the nursery class dressed like lambs—frightened and standing stock still. They were wearing white pillowcases over their heads with holes cut out for their faces and the corners tied up for ears. Cotton balls were glued all over them like white wool, and their noses were painted black.

"What a cute idea for little lambs," Gracie whispered to J.T., and he nodded his head in agreement.

"Victoria makes a pretty little Mary," J.T. whispered back to Gracie.

"Yes, she does. Look at William, though," she giggled,

"he's all feet."

Over to the right of the manger stood William, dressed like an evergreen tree.

His face and feet were the only parts of his body not covered by a heavy dark green foam rubber costume left over from the 80s. He was peering out through a hole, looking solemn and uncomfortable, and his large white tennis shoes were very noticeable.

"Size twelves," someone leaned over the pew and whispered.

"Hey, Marv," J.T. greeted his brother-in-law. He and LaVinia had come in unnoticed and sat down behind them.

"He has a solo," William's mom bragged, "I just hope his voice doesn't crack," she whispered to her brother and sister.

"Shhhhh," Marv admonished the proud mother of his children to be quiet.

Everybody in the congregation was quieting down and focusing on the stage. BevAnn, who was now seated at the piano, began to play. An angel choir, being led by Elizabeth, singing "Hark the Harold Angels Sing," marched in down the center aisle. They carefully took their places between

A Night for Miracles

the manger and William (the tree) on a small set of risers.

Hark, the herald angels sing,

Glory to the newborn king

peace on earth and mercy mild

God and sinner reconciled...

Elizabeth had her auburn hair up in a ponytail, and she did look very angelic in her white robe, with her halo, and wings. Her hands were folded in front of her as if she were in prayer while she sang the loudest of all the angels. When the singing stopped, she nervously stepped down to the microphone and looked out into the crowd. She could only see shadows and silhouettes, but she knew they were all staring back at her and her alone. Her stomach felt tight and funny, but she opened her mouth anyway and said, "Ummm."

The congregation waited for her to say her lines, but Elizabeth, the drama queen, had been smitten with a case of stage fright.

"Ummm," she cleared her throat, trying to remember her part.

Coming from the manger beside her, Victoria prompted her with a faint whisper, "Glory to God in the highest..."

"Uh, oh, yeah. Glory to God in the highest and on earth peace, good will toward men." The audience applauded. She turned to take her place once again at the end of the risers next to her annoying cousin, the evergreen tree. Her face was red with embarrassment. William smiled compassionately at her from within his costume prison, sympathetic to her plight. Suddenly, she felt a kindness towards him that she had never felt before; maybe it was pity.

Next came three little wise men walking down the aisle to the accompaniment of "We Three Kings." Dinky was leading the way, carrying a small treasure chest presumably filled with gold. Gracie smiled at him as he walked by, but he never lost his focus, even when she took his picture. He made his way to the stage and walked straight to the manger like he'd been told to do.

During rehearsals, it had been empty because Miss Patsy couldn't find baby Jesus. Then, just before the play started, she found the pitiful china doll in a Sunday school room closet. It had been used in every Christmas play at Hope Springs Church for the last seventy-four years. It was old and ugly. Most of its hair was gone, and what was left was matted together in one big black clump. Its face was dirty and cracked, but its lips were still, surprisingly enough, bright red. Although it was a frightening-looking thing, Miss Patsy hated to break with tradition, so she wrapped it in a white baby blanket from the nursery and put it in its place.

Dinky solemnly knelt down at the manger, supposing it to be empty, intending to say his part when he saw the ugly and decrepit baby doll lying there.

"Ahaaaaah!" he screamed loudly and frantically—frightened half out of his wits, having seen the horrible china doll that he was not expecting. He jumped up, threw down the treasure chest, and ran towards Elizabeth, knocking her off the risers and into William, knocking him flat on his back. He rolled from side to side, squirming, trying to get up, but couldn't because his arms were pinned down under his heavy costume.

Elizabeth rushed to help her cousin get up, but he was too heavy. When she saw her attempt to help right William was futile, she stepped back into place on the risers. Her halo was crooked, one of her wings was missing, and part of her hair had come down from her ponytail. She stared straight ahead into the audience while Dinky stood beside her, shaking and sniffing uncontrollably.

The other little wise men continued on to the stage

and said their parts loudly, trying to be heard over the frantic lambs who were all crying wildly. Miss Patsy was mortified. She was sitting on the front row across the aisle from Gracie and J.T. with her face in her hands, not knowing what to do.

It was then time for William's solo, which he had practiced for weeks. BevAnn started playing because she couldn't see what had happened on stage, and she didn't know that William was flat on his back and could not get up. He was still rolling from side to side, both of his feet kicking the air, but when he heard the music start, he laid still and came in right on queue with a distant but rich and melodious voice.

> God rest you merry gentlemen,
>
> let nothing you dismay,
>
> remember Christ our Savior
>
> was born on Christmas Day
>
> to save us all from Satan's pow'r
>
> when we were gone astray.
>
> O tidings of comfort and joy,
>
> Comfort and joy;
>
> O tidings of comfort and joy.

A Night for Miracles

"Oh, my dear Lord!" moaned LaVinia, his mother, helplessly. "He's singin' anyway!"

"The show must go on," said Marv in his droll, witty style. His wife balled up her fist and punched him in the top of the arm, giving him her "don't say another word" look.

"Ow," he moaned, rubbed his wound, and slumped down a little lower in his seat.

By the time William finished his song, still on his back, the little lambs were no longer crying, but some were still sniffling. Dinky, shaken and pouting, went to the steps in front of the microphone and sat down. He put his elbows on his knees and his chin in his hands, and, looking out towards J.T., he said in a whiny whimper that magnified throughout the whole church, "Uncle J.T., that wudn't werf five dollars!"

"I can't believe this is happening," Gracie said as J.T. patted her back in sympathy. He wanted to get to Miss Patsy and comfort her, too, but he couldn't leave his sister. From time to time, he would glance over at her to make sure she was alright.

Suddenly, Miss Patsy started shaking uncontrollably, and an ungodly hysterical sort of laughter came pouring out of her. The whole congregation looked towards her in stunned surprise. Pastor Al, who had wanted to laugh for the last few minutes, couldn't hold it in any longer either. He laughed so hard he was making snorting sounds. Then, the entire audience began to laugh uncontrollably, too. Harper Randall took his opportunity and ran onto the stage to stand William upright.

For two or more minutes, the kids on stage had no idea what was going on. They just stood dumbstruck, looking out at their parents, grandparents, aunts, and uncles with wide-eyed confusion until the wild laughter stopped. Then, an eerie silence filled the church as the short little Joseph stepped forward with great determination to say *his* part. He pointed a small outstretched hand towards the manger, just like Miss Patsy had taught him, and with a soft but clear child's voice said, "Behold, the Lamb of God who takes away the sin of the world."

The church was silent for a few seconds. Then, the ladies in the audience who had been laughing so hard now began to sniff, and some of them couldn't hold back tears. They dabbed their eyes and cheeks with tissues and handkerchiefs. The men sat quietly with their heads down and their hands folded because the moment had turned so solemn.

Then, the young pastor stepped to the microphone.

"The Lamb of God," he said with his lower lip trembling, "not just a baby, but a sacrifice. His mother knew it. Joseph knew it. Do you know it this evening? For God so loved the world He gave His only begotten Son that *whosoever* would believe in Him would not perish but have everlasting life."

He stood quietly for a moment, looking out at the congregation.

"What a Christmas present!" he shouted. "What a gift!"

The grownups in the pews and the children on the stage all started to clap wildly. Shouts of "Amen!" and "Praise the Lord!" resounded throughout the church.

Miss Patsy stepped up to the microphone next and started to sing as her mother played the piano with a tear in her eye. The angel choir and the rest of the congregation joined in.

> Joy to the world, the Lord is come!
> Let earth receive her King!
> Let every heart prepare Him room,
> and heav'n and nature sing,

and heav'n and nature sing,

and heav'n, and heav'n and nature sing.

Hope Springs Church had never seen a Christmas play like this one in seventy-five years. People were hugging, shaking hands, and kissing one another on the cheek. Even BevAnn was smiling. Gracie thought that, in itself, was a miracle.

Viney, Marv, and their kids left Apple Muffin Cottage early after their Christmas Eve celebration because Viney had to get her Christmas turkey ready for tomorrow. J.T. headed out soon after, patting his tummy.

"It's been a wonderful Christmas Eve, sis, but I ate too much."

"Christmas Eve comes but once a year, little brother."

"Night all!"

"Night, Uncle J.T., watch for Santa Claus. He's prob'ly nearby." Dinky stuck his head out the door and looked into the night sky.

"Night, Uncle J.T., Merry Christmas." Elizabeth waved.

Gracie tucked the kids into bed and kissed them

A Night for Miracles

goodnight after they'd all listened to Elizabeth read the second chapter of Luke. She closed their doors and, on her way back down the stairs, stopped at the landing and pulled back the curtains at the window. A bright full moon was shining over the yard. Thousands of diamonds shimmered and sparkled in the light.

Maggie had shown her the diamonds in the snow years ago, at this same window, on a cold, clear, moon-bright night like this one. As they stood together watching for Santa's sleigh and listening for jingle bells, they marveled at the glistening jewel-encrusted snow.

The August day Maggie left, little Gracie reminded her that she wanted to see the diamonds in the snow again. Maggie kissed her head and promised she'd show them to her again someday.

Just then, she heard the faint, muffled sound of "Jingle Bells" coming from her jeans pocket. She thought the ringtone would be cute for the season.

"Hello," she said as she answered her cell phone, still looking out at twinkling snow.

"Merry Christmas, Gracie girl." The voice on the other end spoke with a slight Irish brogue. Thirty-two years of pain melted away, and she felt like a little girl again.

"Mama," she said excitedly but in a hushed tone, not wanting to wake the children. "Is that you?"

The caller hung up. It had come from an unknown number.

Gracie wasn't sure if she had just imagined her mother's voice as she gazed at the twinkling diamonds in the snow.

Chapter 15:

Trying to Move Forward

> *"Trust in the LORD with all your heart, And lean not on your own understanding; In all your ways acknowledge Him, And He shall direct your paths."*
>
> **Proverbs 3:5–6 (NKJV)**

Gracie drummed her fingers on the kitchen table in time with the slow dripping of melting snow off her back porch roof while she drank her morning tea. Thoughts scurried through her mind as quickly as little winter birds were snatching their breakfast from the grapefruit rind hung in the holly bush outside the kitchen window. She and Dinky made the homemade bird feeder last week and filled it with peanut butter and birdseed balls.

It was a new day, a new year, a clean slate on which to write new plans and New Year's resolutions. It was a time to move forward. She was trying, but the fibromyalgia was reminding her that it was still there. She tried desperately every day to forget it, but the aching of her hands, feet, legs, neck, back, and shoulders reminded her that this insidious thief was still making itself known, and it made it hard to concentrate.

"Happy New Year!" Elizabeth came through the kitchen with her hair puffed out from around a scrunchy.

"Are your new PJs warm?"

"They sure are, and they feel so soft, too." Elizabeth rubbed her eyes, then stepped forward to hug her mother.

"Good! And Happy New Year to you. What's your New Year's resolution?

"To try as many of Grammy's recipes as I can. Mama, can I get the rest of her recipes out of the attic?

"I don't see why not. I think she put them up there for you anyway." Gracie loved seeing Elizabeth happy and enthused.

"What's your resolution? Do you have one?"

"Several, probably. I resolve to be a better Christian, a good mother, a good sister, a good aunt, and a good friend.

And I resolve to pray more and listen for His answers." Gracie pointed upward.

"Why's that, Mama?"

"'Cause we don't have time to waste trying to figure stuff out on our own."

"That's what Grammy always said. I guess she was right, huh?"

"Yes, indeed."

"Mama, let's open a bakery."

"We need to get Christmas put away before we open a bakery." Gracie laughed. "And today, we have to make cabbage and cornbread for New Year's. It's a tradition in this house."

"We can dream, can't we, Mama?"

"Of course, we can. What will we sell?"

"Pies, cakes, cookies—apple muffins, of course."

"Of course, Grammy's apple muffins!" Gracie parroted.

"I even have a name for our bakery."

"What are we going to call this joint venture of ours?"

Apple Muffin Cottage

"Apple Muffin Cottage Bakery."

"Yes, I love that."

"I've been thinking about some names for our different items like 'A Pinch-of-Love Peach Pie,' 'George Washington's Honest Cherry Pie,' 'Over-the-Hill Prune Danish.'"

"'Cause it makes you run over the hill to the outhouse," laughed Gracie, "I see. You silly kid. Keep that all in mind. Nothing ventured; nothing gained."

"NVNG," Elizabeth agreed.

***

Pastor Al's first sermon of the New Year was very inspiring: lay aside every weight that hinders us so we may run our race and finish our course. Gracie really liked him. He seemed to have a very kind and gentle spirit. She hadn't introduced herself to him yet because she hadn't had the opportunity.

When the service ended and everyone was dismissed, it seemed like it took forever for Gracie to get her children out the door. By the time Elizabeth ran back to her Sunday school room to get her Bible and Dinky picked up his Sunday school papers he'd dropped under a pew, most

Trying to Move Forward

everyone else had gone.

Pastor Al was coming back through the sanctuary from the vestibule and made a beeline for Gracie as they were leaving.

"We were glad to have you with us this morning, Mrs...?" said the young pastor, with his Bible tucked under his arm, wanting Gracie to fill in the blank as he smiled and stuck out his hand to her.

"Hello," Gracie smiled back and shook his hand. "I'm Gracie LeMaster, and I think you are familiar with my children, Elizabeth and Davis." She was glad he seemed so congenial despite the Christmas Eve fiasco.

"What was your name again, please?"

"Gracie LeMaster."

"And your husband's name?"

"Ben LeMaster. But I've been widowed for the past five years."

"Excuse me, ma'am. I have an important matter to attend to." The broad smile left his face as he went inside his office and closed the door, leaving Gracie stunned and speechless.

"Wow. What was that all about?" Elizabeth asked her mother.

"I don't know."

"He prob'ly went in there to talk to God," Dinky added. "That's his boss."

BevAnn, who was still sitting at the piano, had been privy to the entire discourse. She smiled slyly at Gracie, picked up her sheet music, and said with a smirk as she walked away, "Have a nice day."

For days afterward, Gracie wondered if she could have said something offensive to him. Maybe there was a language barrier. Maybe he hadn't heard her right. What had BevAnn been telling him? It just didn't make sense.

***

"Oh no! More snow?" Gracie held the kitchen door open for J.T. as he brought in extra firewood for the old stove.

"Yup, almost the end of January, and we still have a lot more winter left."

"Not a thing we can do about it, I guess. Have some breakfast with me." Gracie passed him a warm apple

Trying to Move Forward

muffin and poured him a cup of coffee. "I'm having coffee today. Tea just won't do it this morning."

"You okay, sis?" J.T. studied his older sister. She looked tired today.

"Oh, yeah, just a case of the winter doldrums. Thanks again for keeping us supplied with wood."

"You're always welcome, Gracie. Hey, I've been thinking about something."

"What's up?"

"I know you've been wondering how you're going to take care of the orchards. Marv and I've been talking, and we're gonna get some help to prune the trees for you next month. We'll get them fertilized in late spring."

"Really? Oh, that's so sweet of you two."

"And I know a lot of the trees are old and won't make it another year. So, I want to plant my fruit trees in the orchards and free up where I'm growing them now so I can build a house on that spot."

"Oh, wow, you've got lots of plans. I can't let you do all that without paying you."

"I have a proposition for you. I'll take over managing

the orchards, and we'll go fifty-fifty on any revenue they make."

Gracie's eyes puddled with tears.

"Oh, my goodness, little brother, you're an answer to prayer."

"I think it's a win-win situation."

"No doubt!" Gracie was so relieved.

Things were moving forward after all.

We're taking care of the fruit, Grammy.

Chapter 16:
Humdrum Days

"To every thing there is a season, and a time to every purpose under the heaven..."

Ecclesiastes 3:1 (KJV)

February came in dull and gray. Farmwell Valley seemed to lie beneath a perpetual sheet of ice and fog caused by the melting and refreezing of old and new snow.

The whole house seemed filled with the smell of apple bread, one of Grammy's favorites, coming from the kitchen. Elizabeth had been baking all morning.

"Hey, Mom, why do I sound like a frog?" Dinky was sitting on the floor playing with his circus toys.

"Because you've had those old sniffles again. Is your throat still sore and scratchy?"

"Not so bad."

"Good." Gracie leaned down, kissed him on the

forehead, and declared he had no fever.

"If you have any more of these sniffles like that, I'm going to take you to the doctor in Brotherton you used to see." She wondered why Dr. Mac—Ian—hadn't set up his practice in Hope Springs yet. According to Doctor Barnes, he should have come in January.

"When can I make a snowman? I'm getting tired a waitin'. Elizabeth promised she'd teach me."

"You've been too sick, sweetie. I might let you go to the bunkhouse later and play video games with Uncle J.T. He asked if you could come over." Her brother seemed a little lonely, too.

Gracie had some cabin fever these days. From time to time, she checked her emails, but there were never many. Sometimes, Michael would just send a *hello*, or Alice would call to tell about her quilting classes. She was helping Gwen make her first quilt. Their church was running smoothly, of course. Michael and the good Lord were seeing to that.

Patsy would forward something on email she thought Gracie might be interested in, but there'd been no word from her for a few days. There had been nothing else from the elusive Maggie O, either. She'd been tempted to send another email to *Timeless Treasures* and ask for her appraisal again, but she thought it best not to *stir the pot*, as Grammy used to say.

Her days were usually filled with taking care of Dinky, teaching Elizabeth, keeping up with the housework, and chatting on the phone some with Viney.

"Hello," Gracie answered the phone.

"Hey, Gracie, how are you guys doing over there?" Viney asked.

"We're good. Dinky is better. No more fever. How are you? You any better at all?"

"Nope, not really. I'm so sick. Can't seem to shake this stomach bug. It's whippin' my butt."

"Oh, golly. What can I do for you?"

"Nothing, thanks. Marv and the kids are taking care of me and things. Long time since I've been this sick."

"Is Amy Patterson filling in for you at the shop?"

"Yes, I'm so glad I brought her on board last summer. She's always a real help."

"Great! Great! Hey, listen, if there's anything I can do

for you..."

"Yeah, sure, yeah, I'll call. Love you."

"Love you, too. Feel better."

Gracie found herself, once again, hoping Ian would soon get to town. He was a good doctor, and Farmwell Valley would be the better for him being here.

"Mama, we need flour and baking powder if I'm going to try that *hummingbird cake*," Elizabeth informed her mother when Gracie stepped into the kitchen. She had retrieved Grammy's recipes from the attic and had been busying herself trying out the different confections. "And cream cheese for the frosting."

"Okay. Add them to my list. We need several things," Gracie sighed. She hated going to BevAnn's store and always put it off until the last minute. Miss Patsy was the only bright spot there.

"I'm going to get your brother ready and let him go play video games with Uncle J.T.; then I'll get my shoes and coat on and head out. What would you like for supper?"

"Pizza sounds good."

"Great, then I won't have to cook," Gracie smiled.

Chapter 17: Meadows' Grocery Store

August 14, 1969

BevAnn Meadows looked out the window of her dad's grocery store towards the gas station across the street. Pete Andrews was having his Corvette gassed up and the oil checked. He was getting ready to leave town after all. She was beyond hurt. Nothing that she said or did had convinced him to stay.

"Please stay," BevAnn asked him last night by a deserted cabin that sat in his uncle's field along the old logging road. Fireflies danced in the trees as well as on the ground all night until the summer sun dawned, and once again, she asked him not to go.

"I have to, but I hate to leave you."

"Someone else?" Pete didn't answer.

"Will you be back?"

"From time to time, maybe, but, BevAnn, I can't promise you anything. And I'm sorry."

If she had meant so little to him, he could go. She'd been hardened by Joshua's rejection anyway. He had been *the love of her life,* and when he came home from New York married to Maggie, it was *the shock of her lif*e. She, along with everyone else in Hope Springs, always assumed they would marry someday. Having grown up together, they were inseparable until he joined the military. Then, there was the crash in Vietnam that took his life... She was numb now and indifferent. For a while, she thought she might even love Pete. He was little more than a stranger to her at the beginning of summer when he first came to Farmwell Valley.

"You're beautiful! And I hear you teach piano," Pete told her the first time they met in the grocery store. He looked at her over the top of his sunglasses. "I play some—a little—piano."

"Thank you, and yes, I do teach piano."

"I was a studio musician for some rock bands before Nam." He smiled. His long, curly blonde hair looked good on him. "And I sing a little. We should get together sometime. You sing?"

"A little."

"When?"

"When what?"

"Can we get together?"

She hesitated for a while, but once she did agree to meet him, a summer romance blossomed between the young, sophisticated music teacher and the rock musician with the bell-bottom jeans and sleeveless leather vest. She was intrigued by his bad-boy image and multiple tattoos on his heavily muscled biceps. There was also something mysterious and sad about him she thought she might fix.

"I'm so glad I didn't tell anybody about us," BevAnn whispered to herself. "Nobody knows. Thank God, nobody ever will. There's probably somebody else. Oh, gosh, how could I have been so stupid?"

"What did you say, Bevvie?"

"Nothing, Dad. Never mind. It's nothing." As she stood by the cash register, she found it hard to take her eyes off of Pete.

"Look at that long-haired hippie over at the gas station.

Who is he? Do you know, BevAnn?" Claudia, one of BevAnn's friends, asked her as she came into the store.

"No, Claudia, I don't."

"Wow. Look at that guy! Who is he? Did you say you knew him? You know everybody, BevAnn. He's kinda cute. Or *tuff*, they say nowadays. He's definitely *tuff*," Linda chirped.

"I don't know him, I said," BevAnn snapped. She didn't want to admit that her heart was hurting and she wanted to cry.

"Well, look there. Isn't that Maggie, Joshua's wife? I mean, widow? Poor thing! She really is a beautiful woman," Claudia announced as she saw Maggie step from seemingly out of nowhere off the highway and approach Pete.

BevAnn took a longer look, more curious than ever, as Maggie got closer to talk to him.

"Hum, looks like she knows him." Linda was staring at them. "Look how close they are."

All eyes in Meadows' Grocery were fixed on the couple across the street.

Meadows' Grocery Store

Pete opened the passenger's door for Maggie.

"Well, I'd never believed it if I hadn't seen it," Claudia said with surprise.

From the window of Meadows' Grocery BevAnn's friends and BevAnn were shocked as they watched Maggie ride away with Pete.

BevAnn was no longer numb. Anger rose up in her like a fiery dragon.

Chapter 18:
Meadows' Grocery – Your Friendly Neighborhood Store – 2002

Sure, so very friendly, Gracie thought as she pulled up in front of the only grocery store in town and once again read the big sign that hung above the huge windows facing the highway:

Meadows' Grocery—Your Friendly Neighborhood Store

From inside the store, BevAnn—blue knit pantsuit on, matching heals, perfect hair, and flawless makeup—

watched Gracie get out of her Jeep. Directly behind Maggie Barton's daughter, across the highway, was an empty lot where the old gas station was in the late 1960s until it was torn down in the early eighties. The thought of what happened that day still brought back hurtful memories.

"Hey, Miss LeMaster."

"Hello, Harper. Where's Miss Patsy today?" She said as she steered her grocery cart past the store's office and didn't see her friend.

"She's down with the flu. She hasn't been in for a while."

"I'm so sorry to hear that. I'll have to make her some chicken soup."

"Harper, don't you have something to do?" BevAnn demanded of the stock boy.

"Yes, Ma'am," Harper said as he grinned at Gracie and went about his business."

BevAnn looked past Gracie as if she wasn't there as she walked on, but that was the usual routine in Meadows' Grocery unless Miss Patsy was there for a quick, friendly chat.

"Good for the body and good for the soul, I'm told," someone said in a deep male voice while leaning over her shoulder.

"Ian! We've been expecting you. Dr. Barnes told us you were taking over his practice. How are you? It's good to see you." Gracie blushed when she saw him. She always felt tongue-tied and awkward around this handsome middle-aged doctor. He wrapped both his arms around her and gave her a big hug.

"I'm good. Yourself?" He was a tall, slender man with dark hair and hazel eyes shadowed by glasses. "It's good to see you, Gracie."

"I'm doing okay." She couldn't think of anything else to say as she tucked her hair behind her ear and smiled at him. She noticed his hair and mustache had gotten a little whiter since she had seen him last. He looked very distinguished and smelled of cologne and leather.

"Hey, you're just the person I needed to see."

"Oh, really? Why's that?"

"I need some help getting my computer set up and my programs loaded for my practice. Think you'd have the time? I pay good."

"Let's barter," she said to him, somewhat bolder than she meant to.

"What do you have in mind?" he asked her teasingly. Gracie blushed again.

"How about some free office visits for my kids, maybe?"

"Oh, hello, pastor." Ian recognized Pastor Al as he unexpectedly walked past with his grocery cart.

"Good afternoon, doctor," the young minister answered and smiled.

"Hello, Pastor Al," Gracie added cordially, but he passed her without acknowledging her greeting. When he ran into BevAnn an aisle ahead, they whispered and glanced back at her.

Gracie reddened even more from humiliation.

"I can sure do that. Can you start Wednesday? Gracie, can you come in Wednesday?"

"Yes, I can." Gracie was glad to resume her conversation with a trusted friend.

"Ten o'clock?"

"Ten o'clock. I'll be there."

Gracie brought her groceries home along with an extra large pepperoni pizza from the Pizza Stone, which was next door to Meadows' Grocery. Her emotions were mixed. Seeing Ian again brought joy to her heart, but she was stunned by the rudeness of Pastor Al. His discourtesy to her warranted an explanation. She would have to call him.

J.T. brought Dinky home, stayed for pizza, a kid's movie, and then carried his little nephew to bed. Elizabeth followed them upstairs and said goodnight. The wind had kicked up and was howling through Spirit Creek Farm like a banshee when Gracie saw J.T. out the backdoor to go to the bunkhouse.

"Listen, Gracie. Do you hear it?" J.T. asked her as he stepped outside.

"Oh, I do. Are you washed in the blood, in the soul-cleansing blood of the lamb? I hear it." Gracie recognized the tune the soft violin played as it intertwined with the night wind.

"Where in the world is that coming from?"

"Old Jacob Barton, when the Civil War was startin'…"

Apple Muffin Cottage

Gracie said as she grinned and patted her brother goodnight. He put his hood over his head, stuffed his hands in his pockets, and headed for the bunkhouse laughing.

In the quiet of Apple Muffin Cottage's kitchen, Gracie found herself very troubled after J.T. left. For the first time in a long time, she found herself missing Ben. She knew Elizabeth missed him more than she liked to admit, but they couldn't seem to talk about it. What would he think if he knew she was having feelings for Ian?

Dinky's and Viney's health both worried her. She didn't dare tell her sister anything about their mother right now. Her sweet friend, Miss Patsy, was sick. Pastor Al and BevAnn hated her for some reason. Then, there was the mysterious person haunting Spirit Creek Farm with soul-tugging hymns from their pasts.

"Oh, Father God, help me tonight," she said as she prayed at the kitchen table like Grammy always did. She picked up her Bible, and it fell open to Luke 10:41:

"…Martha, Martha, you are worried about many things."

It comforted her to know that the Lord heard her prayer, knew her heart and what was on her mind tonight. *Yes, many things, Lord.*

Surprisingly, when she checked her emails before going to bed, there was one new message, and it *was* from Maggie O. Gracie hesitated to open this *Pandora's Box*.

Gracie,

Why seek ye the living among the dead?

Maggie O

Gracie was staggered, and her heart was gripped with compassion for her mother as she read the words from the 24th chapter of Luke.

Chapter 19:

Hope Springs Eternal

Blessed is the man who trusts in the LORD, And whose hope is the LORD.

For he shall be like a tree planted by the waters...

Jeremiah 17:7–8 (NKJV)

Between a very large silver maple and a huge ash tree near the top of Crown Ridge, a spring bubbles up from an unknown underground source. Its cold, clean, gushing water found its path of least resistance years ago, ran down the steep hill, and spilled over a six-foot rock ledge, creating a continual waterfall that eventually carved out a small shallow pool.

From there, it poured over smooth rocks and small boulders, continuing on its downward path. It mingled with other rivulets and minute tributaries from atop Crown

Ridge, eventually forming the headwaters of Spirit Creek, which snakes and meanders throughout Farmwell Valley.

Deer, other small animals, and pioneers going west found the little place to be a refuge. Some decided there was no need to travel further because they felt at home. Quickly, a settlement sprang up around the little waterfall fed by the spring. In 1793, a young circuit riding preacher, who came through regularly but decided to put down roots, named the little town Hope Springs. With the help of the Isaiah Barton family, other nearby landowners, and settlers, he built the first Hope Springs Church.

Old Jacob Barton's grandfather, William, provided the land directly across the road from the church for the Hope Springs Eternal Rest cemetery in 1812 and enclosed an acre with a six-foot high brick and mortar wall and an iron gate. His parents, Isaiah and Mary, were the first buried there.

Over the years, the forests in the area were gleaned for much of their hardwood, which left behind cleared rich farmland that was soon to become known to many far and wide as Farmwell Valley.

By the time the railroad came through in 1886 (which provided a way to ship the timber out even quicker along with the Bartons' apples), lumber bosses and railroad executives needed housing. So, there were mansions built where old log cabins once stood, and dirt streets were paved with bricks.

For a while, it was a thriving, bustling place. Millinery establishments, boot and shoe stores, blacksmith shops, barber shops, saddle shops, and a hotel filled Church Street. Along with a general store, a tailor, a watch repairman, a butcher, a lawyer, and a doctor, the townspeople had access to most of what they needed. The Hope Springs Sentinel newspaper advertised it all.

Around 1925, the old church burned down, and a new church was soon raised in its place. This time, a small parsonage was erected adjacent to it on its west side.

After most of the hardwood was harvested from the land and the railroad was completed, Hope Springs nearly faded into obscurity. During the two world wars, some industries moved in and then out again. Smaller houses were built, and brick streets paved over with asphalt. Blacksmith shops turned into service stations, and years later, a post office was built, a grocery store, a new doctor's office, a couple of schools, and a pizza parlor known most recently as the Pizza Stone.

Apple Muffin Cottage

Where Miss Patsy lived was known to all in Hope Springs as Melody Manor because it was the home of both the piano and voice teachers in town: her and her mother. It was a large three-story Victorian that sat to the east of the church. To the east of Melody Manor was another large three-story mansion that had been renovated into four very nice apartments (Dr. Mac had recently moved into one). Beyond it, at the very end of Church Street, was a small City Park where the waterfall continued to roll over the rock ledge and into the small pool.

Patsy's bedroom, on the third story of Melody Manor, overlooked the cemetery across the street. Its name was woven into an arched wrought iron sign over an iron-hinged gate at the entrance. The majority of the enclosed tombstones had crosses carved in their fronts and were reminders that most who lived and died in Farmwell Valley were of the Christian faith.

There was a tall spire-like monument in the center of the cemetery commemorating the glorious dead from Farmwell Valley who'd been lost in battle for their nation. Joshua Barton's name was added in 1970, but his body was never recovered. His parents' graves were a couple of rows over. Thomas and Grace Barton rested in peace together under a shared headstone that read:

Hope Springs Eternal

Loving Father and Mother,
Grandfather and Grandmother

John 3:16

Strange things had been occurring within the cemetery's walls for several months. Patsy would hear muffled sobs in the night or the hint of a violin nearby. Then, some days, whole apples were found on headstones and around the veteran's monument. At times, after heavy snows during the night, the cemetery would be filled with a maze of footprints at sunrise.

In the early hours of Wednesday morning, she had a fever, her teeth chattered, and her hands and feet were cold. She had coughed and wheezed throughout the night and, even with her head propped up on two pillows, found it hard to breathe. At 2:00 a.m., she got up to take her temperature and, while waiting for the thermometer to beep, heard the cemetery gate screech, so she peered out her bedroom window into a night made almost as light as day by a platinum three-quarter moon.

A slight wind swirled loose snow around the gray headstones, and she thought for a brief moment that she saw a dark hooded figure float over the ground but concluded, however, that it was due to slight delirium because she had such a high fever. Therefore, she dismissed it, took a pain reliever, along with some cough medicine, and went back to bed.

Chapter 20:

Working for Ian

Arise, shine, for your light has come…

Isaiah 60:1 (NIV)

Five miles away on Spirit Creek Farm, Gracie sat quietly in the wee hours of the morning, staring out her kitchen window, watching a gray, misty fog slowly appear over her snow-laden pasture field. She had seen 2:00 a.m. come and go, too, on the clock on her nightstand before she fell into a half-awake dreamlike stupor. Tossing and turning through the night, her body stiff and aching, she finally got up, put on her robe and slippers, and came downstairs to the kitchen to pray. She heard the soft chimes of the mantel clock in the living room sound five times just as she grabbed an empty tea kettle. It was going to be a long day.

At 9:00 a.m., Gracie called the parsonage but didn't get an answer. By 9:30 a.m., Gracie parked her car at the end of Church Street and walked towards Melody Manor. It was

Apple Muffin Cottage

a large blue mansion built in 1887 for a lumber boss and his wife. It had a wraparound porch surrounded by white columns, banisters with turned spindles, and lots of dental molding that adorned all its edges. In summer, it was filled with pots of red geraniums and white wicker furniture, but in winter, the gray-painted porch was completely bare, except for a lone jute welcome mat. BevAnn's family had bought the house fifty-some years ago, and it had always been kept in pristine condition. She inherited it when her father died, as well as Meadows' Grocery.

Gracie climbed the three concrete steps, being careful of slippery ice, and rang the doorbell. To her surprise, Pastor Al opened the door.

"I was just leaving!" The young minister was very terse with her.

"Thanks for stopping by, pastor." Miss Patsy's voice was raspy and hoarse. "And thank you for the banana pudding."

"You're welcome. I'll check on you tomorrow." He walked past Gracie with his head down, not willing to meet her gaze.

Miss Patsy was standing at the door with her hair pinned up on her head, wearing a jogging suit.

"Hi, Gracie. Pastor came over to check on me. He's been over every day since I got sick. He's a very caring person. And so sweet."

"Really? I haven't had a chance to get to know him yet. So, how are you? I made you some chicken soup."

"How sweet, Gracie. I'm still running a slight fever. You might not want to get too close."

"I just came to drop this off. Dr. McVicker's in town now. His office isn't open yet, but if you need him, I'm sure he'd see you."

"I'll give this another day or so. You know, let it run its course."

"Take care of yourself."

"I will. J.T.'s been calling. I appreciate that."

"Yes, I know. He's been concerned about you."

"Very nice of him."

"Well, you take care and call us if you need anything."

"Thanks again, Gracie. I will. Mom's been taking good care of me. Bye."

At ten o'clock, Gracie was standing outside the

doctor's office on the icy sidewalk, looking at the new sign that read:

Dr. Ian McVicker, M.D.

Family Practioner

Board Certified

For many years, Dr. Barnes' shingle had hung over the door. She missed him terribly and wondered how he was doing in his retirement. Dr. Mac would be good for the town now. She was certain of it.

"Good morning! Ready to go to work?"

"Good morning, Dr. Mac."

"Ian to you, Gracie." His voice was tender, like always. He thought she looked pretty, with her cheeks reddened by the cold.

"Good morning, *Ian*."

She waited for him to unlock the door.

"Ian, what do you think of Pastor Al?"

"Nice guy." Ian turned the key in the lock and pushed hard with his shoulder.

"Do you find him friendly?"

"Very."

Gracie was afraid to say anything else for fear of sounding paranoid.

"But I've noticed he's not so very nice to you. I saw how he treated you at the grocery store Monday. And when I was walking by the Meadows' house, going to the post office a few minutes ago, I saw him totally blow you off."

"Oh, Ian, I don't know what I've done to make him not like me." Her eyes welled up with tears.

"What makes you think you've done anything?"

"For what reason would he dislike me? And quite frankly, I could use a pastor right now, but I guess that's out of the question."

"Gracie, we've known each other for a long time. Come on in. Get warm. Talk to me."

"Oh, Ian, I've got to talk to somebody. I'm just about ready to explode with all of this."

"Let's hear it. What's got you so shook up?"

"It's so many things. I don't know where to begin. Pastor Al is treating me like I have the plague. I'm really concerned about my sister LaVinia. She's been so sick.

And Dinky is just not himself these days."

"Dinky? What's wrong with Dinky?"

"I just don't think he feels very good. He's listless and grouchy. He often has a sore throat. Every now and then, a fever."

"Bring him in and let me check him over."

"And the fibromyalgia doesn't make things easy. I hurt and have a hard time sleeping." Gracie started to giggle a bit. "I feel strange telling you all of my troubles."

"Something more is bothering you, though. I know you."

"Oh, Ian. Yes. Something so big that I can't tell anybody about it yet until I'm certain?"

"Certain about what?" He pulled out a chair for her. She sat her briefcase on a table, took off her coat and gloves, and sat down.

"Do you remember I told you once about my mother and how she left us after my dad got killed? There were four of us. There was me, my brother Michael, my sister Lavinia, and J.T., who was just a few weeks old. She just left us and never came back."

"I remember."

"We haven't known for all these years if she was alive or dead."

"Right."

"Well, Ian, she's alive. I've found her," Gracie whispered, almost afraid for the walls to hear.

"No."

"Yes. I've talked to her through email and once—Christmas Eve—on the phone." Gracie nodded her head to assure him. "I thought until the other day I was imagining all this. Then I got the latest email from her. I need to answer it some way, but I don't know how. I haven't told a soul about it but you. I was too afraid. I've kept all this quiet for the last two months."

She told him how she'd found the quilt top, picture, and letters in Grammy's closet, revealing that Grammy knew Maggie was alive and had been in a mental hospital.

"I think your mother had postpartum depression. From what you tell me, she was a classic case. Several children in close succession, a newborn, then the shock of losing her husband. It was too much. It's a shame. We can treat it so much easier these days."

"I knew there must have been something terribly wrong with her for her to leave us. From what I remember, she always seemed to love us, and we were happy."

"Tell me about the emails again."

She repeated the story of how she inquired about the tea set on the *Timeless Treasures* website and how Maggie O had answered her.

"Mama had written her name on the inside of the box lid when she was little. I took a picture of the tea set and placed the box in the background with only part of her name showing, hoping she would take the bait. And she did." Gracie smiled proudly.

"Let's get your computer hooked up. After all, that's what I've come here to do. Then I'll show you." Gracie worked until half past noon, then yelled at Ian to come take a look at the emails.

"This is wild, Gracie. It's got to be your mom."

"I know. But now the ball's in my court. How do I answer that?" Gracie pointed to the computer screen and read, "Why seek ye the living among the dead?"

"How am I supposed to answer that, and what if I scare her away?" Gracie sighed.

"Gracie, where there's life, there's hope, right? You know that."

"Yes, but she has been dead to us for so long." Gracie wiped a tear off her cheek.

"But who raised the dead? With Christ, even in death, there's hope. He's the resurrection and the life, remember?" Ian patted her shoulder and smiled at her. She'd forgotten what strong faith he had.

"I know." She paused a minute, and her eyes twinkled with excitement. "I do know what to tell her."

Gracie remembered again her mother saying to her in a thick Irish brogue, "Rise and shine, Gracie, the day's a waistin', girl."

She quickly typed a reply to Maggie from the sixtieth chapter of Isaiah, verse 1:

Maggie,

Arise, shine, for your light has come…

Gracie

P.S. The day's a waistin'…

She hit the send button with tears spilling onto the

keyboard. Ian smiled at her, certain God had given her a perfect reply to Maggie's email. Again, he patted her shoulder.

"Thank you, Ian."

"You're welcome, Gracie. Glad I could help. Now, tell me again about Dinky and your sister."

Chapter 21:

Viney's Condition

"A merry heart doeth good like a medicine…"

Proverbs 17:22 (KJV)

"Hi, Gracie," Viney said in a weak voice.

"Hey, Vi, are you feeling any better?"

"Oh, no, I'm sicker than a dog," Viney answered, sounding very tired. "I can't keep anything down, and I'm so exhausted I can't seem to put one foot in front of the other."

"Dr. Mac's in town now. His office isn't open yet, but I bet he'll see you. I could take you over. I've got to be there at ten anyway to do some more work for him."

"I'll have Marv drive me over," Viney said weakly.

"Good. Meet us there a few minutes after ten. Give

him time to get the office opened up." Gracie was sure Ian wouldn't mind.

"I'm glad you told her to come see me." Dr. Mac's brows furrowed. As he unlocked the door, he was already thinking and starting to diagnose LaVinia from what Gracie told him yesterday.

When Marv arrived with Viney, Dr. Mac took her into the examining room right away. She was very pale, had dark circles under her eyes, and had lost several pounds.

"Thanks for having her come see the doc, Gracie," Marv said as they sat together in the waiting room. "I've really been worried about her. She's sick and miserable, and I can't do a thing right as far as she's concerned. I just want to help her, ya know?"

"I know, Marv. She'll be alright. Dr. Mac will see to that. He's a good doctor."

"So you've known him for a while?"

"About five years. He was the plant doctor at Brotherton Alloys."

"Seems like a nice guy." Marv noticed that Gracie talked about him with sweetness in her voice.

Viney's Condition

"There," Gracie said as she patted her brother-in-law's shoulder, "try not to worry." He was short and stocky. His straight blonde hair and blue eyes came from his Swedish ancestry on his mother's side of the family.

Gracie handed him a magazine and noticed that his freckled hands were wide and his fingernails were stained with dirt, oil, and grease. *Spirit Creek Building and Contracting* was his main business, where he employed J.T., but he loved farming.

The Holleys were hard-working, salt-of-the-earth people. Sometimes, they were at odds, though, over their financial stability, so every now and then, they quarreled.

Gracie loved her brother-in-law dearly. He'd been there for all of them during really hard times. Marv was a superhero in her eyes. He was tough but tender and loved his family and neighbors. At times, he'd work all day, help a neighbor all evening, and stay up with a sick baby at night to let his exhausted wife sleep.

"Pregnant?" They heard Viney yell from behind the closed door. Then they heard her giggle.

"Oh, dear God," Marv sighed, "I should have known." Gracie patted him on the back again.

She laughed with him every now and then until Viney and Ian came out of the examining room.

"Looks like a due date of around October second," Dr. Mac told Marv as he shook his hand. "Congratulations, Dad." Marv just grinned and shook his head. "Of course, we'll have to get you set up with an ob-gyn ASAP, Mrs. Holley, since I'm just a GP."

"Okay, Dr. Mac. Thanks again. I thought I was just starting into real early menopause or dying or something, but a baby never entered my mind. I was never sick with my other two," Viney laughed. She smiled at the handsome doctor and felt like she'd always known him.

"At least I know what's going on. I think I can deal with it better now."

"Try to drink as much as you can. And get a lot of rest."

"I will," Viney answered.

"Doc, what do I owe you?" Marv inquired.

"How about a lot of good publicity? Just give me a good recommendation to everybody."

"Will do. Thanks again."

Viney's Condition

"Goodbye, Gracie." Viney leaned over and hugged her sister.

"Goodbye, sweetie," Gracie said as she returned her hug tightly. "Oh, another baby in the family! How exciting." She wanted her sister to feel good about her condition.

"Give us a while to let it sink in," Marv said, somewhat shocked.

"Come on, stud," Viney said to her husband, "let's go home."

Gracie and Dr. Mac laughed and waved as the Holleys drove away.

"What a relief," Gracie sighed. "Thank you, Ian." There was one of her troubles marked off her list. *And thank You, Lord!*

"I'm buying pizza later," Ian reminded Gracie.

"Sounds great! Let's get to work!" Gracie couldn't keep from smiling.

Chapter 22:

Dinky Makes His Own Fun When Miss Patsy Comes for Tea

"But Noah found grace in the eyes of the Lord."

Genesis 6:8 (KJV)

"Ever since you've found Grammy's recipes up in the attic, you haven't had nuffin' to do wif me, Elizabeth." Dinky sat on the floor between the kitchen and dining room, playing with his wild animals—plastic lions, tigers, and elephants. Every now and then, curious Callie Ann stepped intentionally through his menagerie. He was cranky, coughed every now and then, and wiped his nose on his shirt sleeve.

"I've been busy testing them out to see which ones I'll sell in my bakery someday. It's important."

"Yeah! Too busy to play with me. Let me ask you somfin'. What's more important: me or those old recipes?"

"I'm sorry, Dink. I really am. Don't bug me, please. I've got to get back to my schoolwork after lunch."

Dinky ignored her.

"Stripey the Tiger will now do his deff-defying jump from my hand, through the ring of fire, into the black swimming pool!" Dinky dropped the toy tiger into Pop's old, dirty top hat.

"Wish I really had a Stripey the Tiger, Elizabeth," Dinky whined.

"Mama, can I try this one? It looks really good. *Fudge Brownies*."

Gracie was at the kitchen table checking her emails, looking for anything from Maggie, but nothing was there. Elizabeth showed her the recipe.

"Oooh, I remember those. I don't see why not."

"Great!" Elizabeth smiled uncontrollably. Her dimples were deep, and her green eyes sparkled with joy. "Oh,

Dinky Makes His Own Fun When Miss Patsy Comes for Tea

and look! *Diamonds-In-The-Snow cupcakes.* These look great!"

"I'd forgotten about those. Grammy made them for me. I used to help her make them. You know what I think would be good, Bethie?"

"What?"

"Why don't we have a little Valentine tea party? You could try out some of your new recipes."

"For real? No joke?"

"For real!" Gracie was pleased that she could make Elizabeth so happy. "I tell you what. Pick out two or three of your favorite desserts, and we'll also have a few appetizers."

"Who can we invite?"

"We could invite your aunt Viney and Victoria."

"Can we invite Miss Pasty, too?"

"I don't see why not."

"Can we have some pepper-ernies and cheese chunks and round crackers?" Dinky always looked forward to his favorite snack.

"Sure thing, Dinky boy."

"And can we get some little cute heart plates and pretty napkins?"

"I think so, Bethie, or use Grammy's good china. After all, it would be a tea party. Maybe you could even cut your brownies into heart shapes and sprinkle them with a little powdered sugar. Grammy used to do that for us every Valentine's Day. She would stack two or three together, wrap them in plastic, and tie them with a red ribbon."

"I could also make Grammy's *Pink-Pearl* cupcakes. I'd like to get some really pretty wrappers and pink sugar pearls."

"You make a list of what you need, and I will, too."

"Don't furget my pepper-ernies and stuff," Dinky added.

"Oh, I won't forget your stuff, Dinky. We'll also have to pick a day and time and invite our guests."

"Mama, let's invite Uncle J.T. and Uncle Marv, too."

"And match-make a little bit?"

Elizabeth grinned and shook her head yes.

Dinky Makes His Own Fun When Miss Patsy Comes for Tea

"Well, you know we'll have to invite William, too—it's only fair—can you deal with that?"

"I guess so. At least Gwen won't be here—I hope."

***

The Saturday before Valentine's Day was cold but clear. The sky was blue and cloudless. J.T. got up early to shower and trim his beard. By 11:30, he was dressed and ready to go but realized he had forgotten one thing. So, he patted cologne on the sides of his face and then checked himself out in the full-length mirror.

"Lookin pretty good there, ole J.T. Miss Patsy, you don't have a chance, girl!"

He grabbed his leather jacket, threw it on over his red sweater, and headed out the door, anxious to see the love of his life.

***

Patsy took a long last look in the hallway mirror before she put on her coat. She was almost giddy with anticipation to see J.T. and hoped he'd be impressed. Her long blonde hair looked lovely against the deep red sweater she wore. It paired well with her straight gray skirt and black leather boots. She took a small bottle of her signature perfume out of her purse and sprayed a little in her hair, grabbed her coat, threw her purse over her shoulder, and headed out the door. As she drove to Gracie's house, she sang an old familiar love song.

***

Miss Patsy arrived at Apple Muffin Cottage right after the Holleys.

"Come in, Miss Patsy! Come in. Happy Valentine's Tea Party!" Elizabeth was so excited she trembled slightly.

"The same to you, Bethie! Thank you for inviting me."

"Hello," Viney and Victoria said together and waved to her. Marv and William waved, too, and greeted her.

"Hi, everybody. You all look so nice! Everybody's wearing red today."

"We're glad you could join us." Gracie took her coat and motioned for her to sit down.

"Thank you. It smells so good in here! Oh, and look at all the red hearts and pink and white balloons everywhere. It's beautiful! And look at that gorgeous little tea set!"

"It was my mom's when she was a little girl. It's from Ireland. Viney did the decorations. That's always her job."

Dinky Makes His Own Fun When Miss Patsy Comes for Tea

Gracie gave her sister full credit and was glad that she was feeling well enough to participate.

"You've outdone yourselves."

The Regal Brookshire sat in the middle of the dining room table on the old lace tablecloth, surrounded by a delicious assortment of food, balloons, and cut-out hearts.

"They always do. Hello, Patsy. You look very nice." J.T. had been waiting for her and handed her a china cup full of pink punch. He could feel his heart racing. She was beautiful.

"I'm sure they do. And thank you." She blushed at the compliment and took the cup he offered her.

"Who made all this food?"

"I baked the desserts, Miss Patsy, and Mama made the other things. I made fudge brownies cut out like hearts, and you can put cherry pie filling on top along with whipped cream. There are *Diamonds-In-The-Snow* cupcakes. See, they shimmer with sanding sugar on top of the white icing. And Grammy's *Pink-Pearl* cupcakes she used to make for weddings. Aren't they romantic?"

"I made the pepper-ernies and cheese chunks on them round crackers." Dinky was sitting in the corner of the dining room floor playing circus.

"*Those* round crackers. And I sure did make my usual meatballs and cheese balls. Same ole, same ole, and I'm anxious to eat. Anybody else hungry?"

There was a vegetable tray and a fruit tray and heart-shaped biscuits, too. Gracie was so glad to host this little party, along with Elizabeth, for their family and sweet friend. It had been a long winter so far. Just to have her loved ones around her made her feel at ease for the first time in months. She was also hoping that J.T. and Miss Patsy might get closer today.

"Anybody hear that weird music outside?" Viney had been perplexed by it. "Sounded like a violin. Not sure where it's coming from."

"Several of us have." J.T. nervously put his hands in his coat pockets. "Personally, I think it's old Jacob Barton's ghost," he said, teasing.

"Really?" Elizabeth exclaimed.

"Oh, Mama, I'm scared," Victoria said as she put her head on her mother's arm.

"It probably *is* old Jacob's ghost," said Marv from the corner of the living room next to the fireplace. "Don't you

Dinky Makes His Own Fun When Miss Patsy Comes for Tea

think so, William?"

"It's gotta be him. Who else could it be?" William added.

"Guys, look what you've done. You've scared the girls," Gracie said.

"Well, William is right. Who else could it be but ole Jacob out there fiddlin', wondering where he hid that treasure?" J.T. concluded as a joke.

"It would be nice if we could get in on a little bit of that treasure action," stated Viney.

"What's that old legend, J.T.? You may as well sit down and tell us about it." Gracie relented out of curiosity. Earlier, she'd had Elizabeth set several folding chairs around the living room for extra seating.

"Old Jacob Barton, when the silver war was a startin', hid his family's treasure in the ground, but he couldn't remember where he hid it 'cause he was drunk when he did it, and that ole treasure never has been found," Dinky blurted out with his raspy voice. Gracie spit out her punch, and the room erupted with laughter.

"Dinky!" Gracie shouted.

"That's right! Where'd you learn that?"

"Uncle J.T., William taught me. He's always lookin' for it. Told me to be on the lookout for it, too. Said if we find it, I could have me a real circus and not just these old plastic animals and Callie Ann."

"It don't hurt to look," William added with a sheepish grin.

"That's right, boys. Well, let's see. Legend has it that Isaiah Barton surveyed off some land between Crown Ridge and Angel Point for George Washington. What we know today as Farmwell Valley. Old George paid him in land and some silver for services rendered. They were well-off then. Years later, his grandson Henry sold off some of the land but kept this part—Spirit Creek Farm. Then, ole Jacob built this house and lived off the proceeds of what was left of the money and the silver.

"But back in 1863, a band of Confederates, Morgan's Raiders, was coming through these parts to cross over into Ohio. Jacob was drunk, as usual, got scared, and hid his treasure from the Confederate soldiers. When he got through hiding it, he came back home and wrote down three clues in the family Bible as to where he'd hid it, but when he sobered up and the Confederates were gone, those

Dinky Makes His Own Fun When Miss Patsy Comes for Tea

clues didn't make a bit of sense to him or anybody else. And he never did find that treasure. He still searches for it, though, while he fiddles and wonders where he hid it."

"If I see him, I'll follow him and see where he hid it so I can have me a real circus. I'll always keep lookin' for him."

"That a boy, Dinky." His uncle patted his shoulder and ruffled his hair, but inwardly, he was concerned about the things missing from the garage and the cellar house over the last few months. He was certain they were not being haunted by a ghost but encroached upon by a live trespasser.

"But not today. You don't sound like you feel very good."

"I don't, Uncle J.T., my throat hurts. Mama, can I play with the markers?"

"Okay, but at the kitchen table, and don't make a mess." Gracie bent down to feel his forehead. "I'll get you some medicine in just a bit for that sore throat and fever."

"Speaking of strange things," Miss Patsy added, "I wasn't going to say anything about this, but at times, I've heard the old iron cemetery gate screech on its hinges, and

I've seen some things when I looked out."

"Oh, really? Like what?" Gracie asked from the edge of her chair, knowing that there wasn't a bit of nonsense or foolishness about Miss Patsy. This was something serious.

"Well, let's get our food and come back in here to the living room and you can tell us about it," Viney said, not knowing if she could keep it down but needing to eat. "I want to hear more."

"Marv, please ask the blessing over the food."

"Sure thing, Gracie. Dear Lord, we sure are thankful for this day, this food, and our family and friends. Thank You for our new little Holley that's on the way. Bless this food and the hands that prepared it. In Jesus' name, we pray. Amen."

"Amen. Well, congratulations!" Miss Patsy said, surprised at the announcement.

Marv, Viney, and Victoria grinned, but William just rolled his eyes, somewhat embarrassed.

"These meatballs smell great, Aunt Gracie. And I can't wait to get a cupcake and a heart brownie."

"You're in for a real treat, Vic." Elizabeth grinned at

Dinky Makes His Own Fun When Miss Patsy Comes for Tea

her little cousin.

Everybody filled their plates and headed back to the living room, anxious to hear Miss Patsy's tale.

"So, tell us what you saw," J.T. said, eager to know.

"Well, things started happening a few months back after 9/11. I particularly noticed that because we all seemed on high alert," Patsy said while she balanced her plate on her lap and sipped from her cup of punch every now and then.

"I'll hear that gate open and hear muffled sobs like somebody's crying with a broken heart. I think I must be dreaming or something, but this last time, I knew I wasn't. I was sick with the flu, though, and running a bit of a temperature, but I was awake. I heard the gate open, looked out, and there I saw it, plain as day under a big bright moon—a hooded figure gliding through the snow between headstones."

She had everybody's attention. The whole house was quiet as Patsy explained what had been happening in the Hope Springs Eternal Rest cemetery.

"I've seen footprints at sunrise on new snow that's fallen during the night. I walk through there sometimes— it's so pretty and peaceful most of the time. I've found whole apples, like gifts, left on different graves, mainly Mr. and Mrs. Barton's and around the veteran's memorial."

"Really? How strange!" Gracie said but quietly wondered—*Maggie?*

"Sure is," Viney added.

The room was silent, and everybody was tense at the thought of who might be behind these strange happenings.

Miss Patsy took a moment to set her cup on her plate beside her desserts and took a bite of a cupcake.

Suddenly and without warning, Callie Ann came running from the kitchen with a pink balloon clipped to her tail. *Blub blub blub* it went as she made a bank around the fireplace wall, behind the sofa, under the coffee table, trying to get it off, then across Miss Patsy's lap, sending her china plate and cup crashing to the floor.

Miss Patsy screamed, "Lord, help us!"

"Come back, Stripey!" Dinky yelled with a black marker in his hand.

He had striped Callie Ann several times with wet black marker from her nose, across her head, down her back all the way to the tip of her tail where he'd clipped a helium filled balloon. J.T. jumped up to aid Miss Patsy,

Dinky Makes His Own Fun When Miss Patsy Comes for Tea

but after she realized what had happened and that her purse beside her on the floor was full of chocolate brownie, pink frosting, and cherries, she began to laugh hysterically as all the others looked on, stunned and horrified.

"Oh, Miss Patsy!" Elizabeth cried.

"Patsy, I'm so sorry! Davis Benjamin!" Gracie was furious.

Dinky looked into the living room and carefully put his hand behind his back, hiding the marker and his bottom.

***

Dinky didn't get a spanking, but some medicine and was put to bed. Later that afternoon, as the Valentine Tea guests were leaving, J.T. saw Miss Patsy to her car.

"I always have so much fun when I'm around you and the kids."

"I'm sure glad because other people might not call it fun." J.T. grinned and shook his head. "I've got a card for you. Hope you don't mind."

"Of course not." Patsy opened her Valentine from J.T. slowly.

"I'm sorry I don't have one for you."

Apple Muffin Cottage

"That's okay."

As she read it, she remembered lots of times he'd gotten her Valentine cards when they were in school and sometimes even flowers. Her mother would get so upset at any attention he paid to her that she'd have to hide them, but she was always glad that he chose her to be his Valentine.

"Thank you, you're sweet." Patsy stood up on her toes and kissed his cheek.

"You know I love you," J.T. whispered.

"You know I love you, too," Patricia Dawn Meadows whispered back, put her arms around his neck, and kissed him tenderly. He hugged her tightly, determined now more than ever to *never* let her go.

Chapter 23:

Blasts from the Past

"...Rejoice with me; for I have found my sheep which was lost."

Luke 15:6 (KJV)

"And we have a winter storm warning in effect until 11:00 a.m. tomorrow morning. The rain you are currently seeing in your area will soon change over to snow later in the day as the temperature keeps dropping. Snow will be heavy at times, and we may have accumulations of up to 9–12 inches by morning. Blizzard conditions are likely in most of the viewing area starting around 5:00 p.m.," announced the local weather girl.

Oh, great! Another winter storm was moving in from the Midwest. Pastor Al, cold and restless, got up out of the leather chair in his study and turned off the TV. He'd had enough of winter and was homesick for the tropical warmth of his native Honduras. Maybe someday soon, he could go back for a visit, but not until he had things settled with Gracie LeMaster. Everything in his life was on hold until then.

How ironic that this church needed him, the very place where Ben's widow and children lived.

"A temporary assignment," his presbyter had said. "A favor for an old friend."

"Lord, I know You have brought me here to Hope Springs to fulfill my promise to You," he said to God, "but how can I face Mrs. LeMaster?"

It was a rhetorical question. He knew what he had to do. A still, small voice told him a long time ago that he must confess his guilt to Gracie, and he couldn't put it off another day.

It was only half past one. He was sure he had time to get to Spirit Creek Farm and back before the big storm hit. He'd asked BevAnn Meadows for directions, but she was vague. He hoped he could find his way.

***

For some reason, Dr. Ian McVicker had an uneasy feeling about Dinky. Gracie was supposed to have brought him into the office today, but the winter storm warnings had probably kept her home. Hopefully, Dinky was feeling better, but he didn't want to take a chance.

"Molly," he yelled into the waiting room.

"Yo, Dr. Mac," his young dark-haired receptionist with the nose ring and wrist tattoo acknowledged him as she straightened magazines on the coffee table in the waiting room.

"How many more patients do we have scheduled for today?"

"Just one, doc. Mrs. Greer at 12:45."

"Let's get her in and out of here quickly so you can get home before the storm hits."

"That would be good," Molly answered. "My mom won't be so worried."

Ian wanted to get to Gracie's house before the storm hit to check on Dinky. From the way Gracie described his cough yesterday, it sounded like he had bronchitis, and he didn't want it to get worse. He checked his black bag to see if he had what he needed to treat Dinky and, for good measure, threw in a handful of suckers from a jar on his desk.

Apple Muffin Cottage

***

If Farmwell Valley got the amount of snowfall predicted, they might be snowed in for several days. The thought of it sounded cozy and relaxing to Gracie. Even though there had been snow on the ground for weeks, the roads had been clear. But now, she would have an excuse to stay in, build a fire in the living room fireplace, and curl up with a good book. She and the kids would play board games if she could talk them into it. That is, if Dinky felt better and Elizabeth would give up her baking for a while.

Gracie was surprised to see the snow swirling so fast and furious when she looked out her kitchen window at two o'clock. It looked like a whiteout, and the wind was blowing hard. The ETA of the snowstorm was five o'clock, but it had arrived hours earlier than expected, and, she was certain, harder than expected.

The house felt colder, and Gracie could tell the temperature outside had dropped drastically.

It was a good thing J.T. filled the kindling box and stacked extra firewood on the back porch before he left for Viney's to help Marv for a few days. She had enough wood for a week or more.

Gracie had an uneasy feeling about the storm.

"God help all those out in this blizzard," she prayed. "And provide shelter, warmth, and food for all those in need. In Christ's name. Amen."

She was glad J.T. made an extra trip to the store for her yesterday. He was a good brother who truly had a servant's heart. She was seeing a softening in him, too, towards the things of the Lord. He'd asked her just last week if both their parents had been saved and baptized.

"I know Joshua was because Grammy told me. I don't know about Maggie," she answered.

He seemed to stare into space—lost in thought.

"Okay—eggs, butter, buttermilk, sausage links, and bacon—good. I'll make a pancake breakfast in the morning," Gracie, getting back to the task at hand, said aloud to herself as she checked the contents of her refrigerator while putting back half a head of cabbage and a bag of carrots in the crisper drawer. She had just added some nice carrot slices and the shredded other half of the cabbage to the pot of vegetable beef soup, along with two handfuls of macaroni. It would be a hardy soup for supper and better each time it was reheated. Her soup and an iron skillet full of cornbread she had just put in the oven would be perfect for a couple of days worth of snowed-in meals.

And, even if they lost electricity, they could stay warm and reheat food on Grammy's old wood stove.

"So, there," she said as she took off her apron. "That will do nicely, I think."

"Davis Benjamin," she shouted to her little boy, who had been too quiet.

"Come bring Mama your circus book, and we'll read." She wished she could have gotten him into town today to see Ian, but she was concerned about the severity of the storm on its way.

Earlier, Elizabeth made a large pan of brownies while Dinky whined at her constantly.

"I'm too busy," Elizabeth said. "I have brownies in the oven. Go away and stop bugging me."

"Please, Elizabeth, please. You promised," Dinky kept begging with a croupy voice for his sister to take him outside and teach him how to build a snowman.

"You're too sick, Dink," Elizabeth told her little brother. "Just listen to that cough. There's no way you can go out. Mama didn't even take you out of your PJs today."

"They're not my PJs. They're my long johns, just in

case you'd take me outside in the snow. Please, Elizabeth, please."

"Not today!" Elizabeth snapped. "Mom, make him leave me alone!"

"That's enough, Davis Benjamin! Go find something to do and stop bothering your sister."

"Oo-ka-ay," Dinky said, chin down as he shuffled out of the room with Pop's hat in his hand. Since then, she hadn't heard him for a while. He'd been too quiet.

"Dinky!" Gracie yelled up the stairs. "Get a book and come into the kitchen and we'll read by the stove! Dinky, did you hear Mom?" she shouted but got no response. "Dinky!"

"What's wrong, Mama?" Elizabeth asked Gracie as she came down the stairs.

"Have you seen your brother?"

"No. He's not in his room. I just passed it." Elizabeth realized she hadn't heard or seen him in quite some time either.

Gracie got a funny feeling in the pit of her stomach.

"Elizabeth, check the attic—quickly!"

"Okay, Mama!" Elizabeth ran back upstairs and checked the attic while Gracie continued to check all the rooms on the first floor.

"He's not up there, but it looks like he got the snowman fixins!"

"Oh, good Lord!" Gracie said as she opened the coat closet near the front door. Dinky's boots were gone, but he couldn't reach his coat.

"Lord, please don't let him be lost out in this storm!"

"Oh, Mama, I yelled at him! I was mean to him." Elizabeth ran to her mom for comfort.

"Let's think. Let's think," Gracie said, almost hyperventilating, as she held Elizabeth.

"Dear Lord, dear Lord…help me…help me," Gracie prayed.

Suddenly, Gracie heard a knock at the front door.

"Dinky!" She said with relief as she threw it open.

"No, Mrs. LeMaster, it's just me. What's wrong?" Pastor Al asked with concern.

"Pastor, I need help. I can't find my son." Her hands

were shaking, and her pulse was racing.

"Do you think he's still inside?" He asked, hoping. He had just stumbled in through the snow from the driveway. Once he got inside the yard, all he could see was Apple Muffin Cottage's red front door, and he walked straight towards it, not knowing that Dinky may be outside.

"I don't know."

"Have you searched the entire house?"

"I think so. His boots are missing!" Gracie answered, almost unable to catch her breath.

"We need a plan, but first, let's pray, Mrs. LeMaster. Let's pray that God will send us angels to help us find him."

***

Maggie's email to Pete Andrews

Hi, Pete. I haven't talked to you for so long—the last time was when your dad Bernie passed about four years ago. I hope you're doing well. I'm ashamed I haven't kept in better touch. Since you've urged me for years to go back to the farm, I felt it was only right that I tell you that today I'm going to try. I've been living at Brotherton Arms ever since I left New York City just after 9/11 when my business got destroyed as the towers came down.

I'm heading out and hoping I have enough courage to go all the way into the farm this time. I think I'm ready. I've tried so many times before to get my courage up. I've snuck into Hope Springs several times in the last few months, always at night. I park at the city park so no one sees me or my car and go into the cemetery to pray and see Joshua's name on the monument for courage. Funny, last time I was there, someone had put an apple in front of it, and I've found whole apples on Grammy's and Pop's graves before. The last time I was there, it was so strange. I thought I heard feet walking in the snow outside the cemetery walls and could have sworn I heard Joshua's voice say to me, "Why seek ye the living amongst the dead?" It was like a sign from God because I had emailed that very question to Gracie to get her response.

I've met and talked with Michael at his church here in Brotherton. He has helped me so much. I know it was a shock to him the first time we talked, but he's been so forgiving and loving. Gracie's emails have hinted she would take me back. I've had to make sure. She reached out to me after she found *Timeless Treasures* on the internet. Then I reached out to Michael to test the waters.

I also saw and talked to LaVinia in late November. She

was decorating the lobby of the hotel. She's so beautiful and sweet. Of course, she didn't know who I was. I saw her again in January when she was there taking decorations down. She was very sick. I was concerned and tried to help her. Michael tells me she's expecting her third baby. Maybe I can be of some help coming back home. Thanks for being such a good friend to me all these years. If not for you, I may have ended up in the Ohio River. That was my second option that day. Your selflessness in getting me help cost you Woodstock, which I now know you're glad you missed.

Take good care of yourself. I know you miss Sarah, and so do I. She was a great friend. I wish I could have been there, instead of Ireland, to help her during the ALS. You were a good husband to her. Sorry for the long email. My cell number is the same.

Sincerely,

Maggie

***

"Maggie, Pete here. I got your email and thought I'd call you. How's it going?" The 2001 Lexus allowed her to press a button and talk hands-free.

Apple Muffin Cottage

"Looks like I don't have any choice, Pete. The weather has turned bad. I'm on Rt. 25 south of Hope Springs, right at the farm road, in a total whiteout. I *have* to head towards Spirit Creek Farm. I can't see a thing. There's no going back now." Maggie squinted hard to see through her snow-smeared windshield as the wipers smacked back and forth.

"Call me later. I'll be concerned."

"I will."

"Prayers, Maggie, and be careful."

"Thanks, Pete, I have to concentrate on this road," said the petite older woman who, in spite of her age and her eyeglasses, was still beautiful. Her thick shoulder-length hair was no longer naturally dark red but dyed a warm auburn and cut around her face, framing it like a portrait. She wore just a slight bit of makeup—a light foundation, a dusting of blush, a bit of cocoa plum lip color, a small amount of mascara—to bring out the green in her eyes.

"You bet."

He was uneasy for Maggie. Ever since he had given her a ride out of town thirty-two years ago to Brotherton Mental Hospital, he knew it would be difficult for her to return to Spirit Creek Farm. When she stepped off of the highway onto the old gas station's lot that day and told him she needed a ride to New York City, he saw desperation in her eyes. He'd seen it before in so many of his friends who had served with him in Vietnam. He questioned her again about where she really wanted to go. She broke down and said she needed help, so he took her to the hospital. He and Sarah, his late wife, became protective of her and tried to help her regain her mental and emotional soundness. They even sent her back to Ireland to her parents, where, as their only child, she became their caretaker until they passed away and she inherited *Timeless Treasures*, their family business. Her first step back to her children was to sell everything in Dublin and restart her business in New York City.

He hoped in time, her family would accept her back, and he hoped she was ready.

"I guess now's your chance, Maggie O, and I hope it works out for you, hon." Pete was always tender and caring towards her, like a brother she'd never had.

"Me, too. I just hope I can get there."

***

"Thank God," Maggie whispered when she saw that another vehicle had recently gone ahead of her and left tracks in the snow. She followed them until she realized she was pushing the heavy, wet snow instead of driving over it. It was impossible to take her car any further. She would have to walk back in the same way she walked out in 1969. Her fur-lined boots, long dark hooded coat, and thick gloves would keep her warm enough until she got inside. She grabbed her purse and opened the car door with determination.

"Help me, please, Lord," she prayed, "to find my way." Just then, the old fence that bordered Spirit Creek Farm came into view. She'd counted and memorized each picket the day she left. No doubt many had been replaced, but they would guide her home.

The snow was swirling furiously around her, and the wind was taking her breath. The drifts were getting deeper, and it was getting harder for her to pick up her feet, but as the pickets descended, she knew exactly where she was. Just a few feet down the small incline was where the old coal pile used to be. In her mind's eye, she saw a picture of long ago.

Suddenly, she could make out the dark roof line of the old garage that sat on the other side of the driveway, and just slightly beside that, she could see a dark-colored vehicle, or maybe two. Somewhere between where she was now and those two cars was the gate that led to the front yard. With all of this snow, how would she ever get it opened? She grabbed hold of the next pickets, one by one, stepping carefully in and out of the huge snow drifts as she made her way through the maze of white.

Halfway down, a large black object below caught her eye. Could it be a large chunk of coal? Maggie didn't think that anybody still burned coal in this day and age.

"What in the world?" she shouted loudly into the wind.

There, up against the picket fence where the old coal pile used to be, sat a small boy with an old black top hat down over his face. He seemed asleep with a canvas drawstring bag held tightly in his fist.

"Wake up, darlin'! Where's your coat? You'll freeze to death out here!" she said when she reached him.

"Don't take it," the little boy yelled, "don't take it!"

Maggie realized that he didn't know where he was and that he was not well. His bright red cheeks and chin were all she could see of his little face.

"Come with me, little fella!" Maggie shouted to be heard above the endless howl of the wind. He was frightened and dazed. She helped him up to his feet and took the black hat off his head. His blue eyes were glassy, and he struggled to pull away from her.

"It's my hat!"

"Alright. You hold onto that hat, and I'll hold onto you," she yelled. He put the little bag into the hat, determined to keep them both. She threw her purse over her shoulder, picked him up, and discovered there was no longer a gate there but an open pathway through the yard. Directly ahead, through the swirling blizzard, she couldn't see a thing except white and maybe a hint of red. She stood still, afraid to go forward.

"Dinky! Dinky! Follow my voice." Gracie was yelling to her son from the porch. It reminded Maggie of a Bible verse that she'd learned years ago at Hope Springs Church: "My sheep hear my voice, and they follow it."

"Keep yelling, whoever you are," she said into the wind, "so we can find our way."

She then heard a young girl's voice and a man's voice both calling, "Dinky! Dinky!"

Maggie couldn't yell anymore because the wind kept taking her breath, but she started walking towards the sound of the voices and the old farmhouse.

Blasts from the Past

Gracie couldn't believe her eyes as she stood on the front porch looking out into the curtain of white when suddenly, a figure in a dark hood emerged carrying her son.

"Dinky! Dinky!" His mother yelled as she ran towards him and took him in her arms. "Oh, thank God. Thank God." Gracie kept repeating. "Let's get you inside."

"Looks like God sent us an angel," Pastor Al said as he took Dinky from Gracie to carry him inside.

"Not an angel, darlin'. Just me," Maggie said with an Irish lilt.

"Mama, you're home!" Gracie gasped as she grabbed hold of her mother's arm.

***

"Where's Pop's hat?" Dinky wanted to know.

"I have it," Maggie answered.

"Are you a angel?"

"I don't think so," Maggie said and smiled.

"Yep, 'cause you don't gots wings or a halo."

"I'm not so sure about that," Gracie said as she smiled at her mother.

"I smell cornbread," Dinky said weakly. "Did Elizabeth make cornbread?" Everybody in the room laughed, mostly out of relief.

"I'll get it, Mama," Elizabeth said as she ran into the kitchen and took her mother's cornbread out of the oven and sat it on a tile trivet on the kitchen table. Then she sat down in Grammy's old chair and patted on the edge slightly. Callie Ann took her queue and jumped up from her place in front of the old stove and into her lap. Elizabeth hugged her little friend tightly as tears rolled down her cheeks.

"Callie Ann, my little brother's okay," she whispered to Thomas Henry's sister, "and you know how much a brother can mean to you."

"Meow," replied Callie Ann. "Meow."

Chapter 24:

Promises Kept

"For as many as are the promises of God, in Christ they are (all answered) "Yes." So through Him we say our "Amen" to the glory of God."

2 Corinthians 1:20 (AMP)

A hard knock shook the front door of Apple Muffin Cottage.

"I followed somebody's tracks in on the road, then I found a stranded car with New York plates, but I couldn't find anybody," Dr. Mac announced with concern as he let himself in.

"Then, I followed the fence in until I got a glimpse of that red door. Everything alright here?"

"We had a scare with Dinky. He was lost in the snow, but Maggie found him." Gracie was proud that her mother was home. So many times she had confided in Ian about

Apple Muffin Cottage

her, and now she could introduce them.

"Maggie?" That explained the abandoned Lexus.

"Dr. Ian McVicker, meet my mother."

"I'm very glad to meet you, Maggie." Ian nodded toward the lady sitting by the fireplace. He could never have imagined having this opportunity but certainly was pleased for Gracie. He couldn't hide his surprise and kept nodding and smiling at her.

"Doctor," Maggie stood up to shake his hand, "I know I'm a total surprise to everyone."

"A very pleasant surprise," Ian stated.

"Thank you," Maggie said, grateful for the pleasantries.

"I was concerned about Dinky, Gracie. I promised you I'd check him over."

"He's sleeping peacefully now."

"He's got a pretty high fever, though," Dr. Mac surmised.

"I know. He decided to go outside in just his long johns and boots without telling me and got lost in that whiteout. Maggie found him outside the fence holding on to Pop's old black hat. It was a bonafide miracle because we had no idea where he was."

"Yes, indeed, it was Mrs. LeMaster." Pastor Al was glad that he had followed the prompting of the Lord to come to Spirit Creek Farm. He'd been some help to her.

"I'd say so, too. In that whiteout, without that black hat, you may never have found him. I couldn't see my hand in front of my face. I was thankful for the tracks and the fence to guide me in. He must have had a little delirium from the fever," Ian said.

"We're grateful you both made it in. Since nobody knew you were coming, we wouldn't have looked for you had you gotten lost," Pastor Al said. "Me, either, for that matter."

"Hello, pastor. I'm surprised to see you here, too."

"Hello, doctor."

"Gracie, was that J.T. I saw walking off the porch as I came in?"

"No. He's at Viney's helping Marv."

"Well, I just saw a blur. I really couldn't see much of anything." He downplayed seeing a man in an army field jacket and a cap step off the porch after having peered into the living room window. He'd definitely seen someone, but it wouldn't be necessary to alarm the others. There was a man seen walking through town earlier in the week that fit his description who was carrying a violin case and was wearing a large backpack. And there'd been some reports of a possible trespasser on some properties. Things had been reported missing. Hopefully, whoever it was—likely a homeless veteran—found shelter—maybe in the barn or the cellar house until they could move on.

"I'm glad you're here, Ian. Pastor Al carried Dinky into the house, and I changed his wet clothes. We laid him next to the fire to keep him warm."

"Don't worry. He'll be alright. Let's get him undressed and cool him down. I think he's a little too warm."

"Thank God you're here, Ian," Gracie said again with relief.

"I promised you I'd take a look at him. I had to keep my promise." He smiled and winked at her and continued to examine Dinky.

"Looks like both ears are infected, and we have some bronchitis going on. I'll give him a shot—an antibiotic—and something for the fever. He'll be okay, Gracie. You can take a deep breath now."

"I'll try." Suddenly, her knees felt like jelly, and she was exhausted.

"Mrs. LeMaster, is there anything I can do?" Pastor Al noticed she seemed weak and pale.

"Just continue to pray for my son," Gracie said, smiling. "I'm glad you're here, too."

"I am, also," answered the young minister. She felt a slightly familiar connection to him that she could not explain and wondered what he wanted and why he had come here.

Maggie got up and stood silently by the dining room doorway with her arms folded across her chest, her purse on her shoulder and stared at the floor.

"Maggie, Mama, please make yourself comfortable," Gracie addressed her lovingly, "come back and sit down." The last time they'd been in this room together, her mother told her she was going to New York City to find her daddy. Five-year-old Gracie asked her if that's where heaven was and if she was going there, too. She'd seen her lay something on Grammy's sewing basket. Ah! Her quilt top!

"Thank you," said Maggie, taking off her coat.

Elizabeth came through from the kitchen with a tray and set it down on the coffee table. She handed her grandmother a cup of hot chocolate and smiled at her sweetly, noticing how much they looked alike. She thought she was beautiful. Maggie smiled shyly at her.

"Pastor Al, hot cocoa?"

"Thank you, Elizabeth," he said, reaching for the cup.

"You're welcome," she answered and then served a cup to Ian and her mother.

"I heard you come in, Dr. McVicker."

"Thank you." He smiled at her and took a sip. He seemed nice. She knew her mother liked him, and she could see why.

Gracie looked at her gratefully through misty eyes and thanked her.

"I'm glad everything's okay, Mama," Elizabeth whispered.

"Me, too, Bethie, me, too."

The blizzard continued throughout the rest of the evening, dumping snow on Farmwell Valley. Mounds of snow continued to pile up in drifts around the house and all of the other structures on Spirit Creek Farm while strong winds blew and shook the windows of Apple Muffin Cottage. With the exception of Dinky, all of its occupants had a supper of soup and cornbread around the living room fire.

Around nine o'clock, the power went out. By the amber glow of the fireplace, Gracie made her way to the half door underneath the staircase in the hallway, where she found several flashlights and batteries.

"Mrs. LeMaster, let me help you with those." Rev. Al took the things from Gracie's hands.

Earlier, she'd made up beds for all her guests. There were two cots in the living room for Ian and Pastor Al next to Dinky, and there were clean sheets on Dinky's bed for Maggie.

"Mom, your cell phone is ringing!" Elizabeth yelled soon after the lights went out. She handed Gracie her phone.

"How you doing? Did you lose power? We just did. And phone service has been out for a while now, too." It was J.T.

"Yeah, power's out, but we're fine. You're not going to

believe what happened here today, and you won't believe who's here."

"Maggie," J.T. answered flatly. Gracie was dumbfounded.

"How did you know?"

"Michael called me earlier this afternoon before the blizzard started. He's been in contact with her secretly for a while now, trying to help her come home. Apparently, she called him when she started for the farm. I didn't want to say anything to you just in case she backed out.

"Wow! Well, how's Viney with all of this?"

"It's a big shock to all of us, but we'll adjust. She's okay."

"Good. So, I guess you'll be there for a while, huh?

"A couple of days, probably. Have Bethie put some wood in the stove."

"Don't worry about us; we have some help. Pastor Al and Ian are here and snowed in, too. I have lots more to tell you when you get home. Love you!" Gracie felt like her brother was on the moon tonight, so near but yet so far away.

"Elizabeth, would you put some more wood in the kitchen stove?"

"Sure, Mom."

Gracie was glad the heat would rise and warm the second floor. *Thank God for Grammy's old wood stove.*

At about ten o'clock, the storm stopped, and the night sky cleared.

"Maggie, I know you're exhausted," said Gracie, "let me show you to your bed." Maggie slowly followed Gracie up a very familiar stairway. As they passed the window on the first landing, a full silver moon shone on the huge drifts, making them sparkle.

"Look, Gracie," Maggie stopped, "do you see the diamonds in the snow?" Gracie shook her head yes but found it hard to speak for holding back tears. She reached out and took her mother's hand.

"I remember the diamonds in the snow, Mama. You promised me you would show them to me again one day. Somehow, deep inside me, I always believed you would. Thank you, and thank you for saving my son's life." Gracie sobbed as she threw her arms around her mother's neck.

"I'm so sorry I left you," Maggie cried.

Apple Muffin Cottage

***

Morning dawned cold and still. Every now and then, a tree branch broke from the weight of the heavy snow and sounded like the crack of a rifle.

Once again, there were Grammy's apple muffins for breakfast, thanks to Elizabeth, who'd baked some a few days ago and warmed them up in the warming drawer of the old stove. Pancakes would have to wait until tomorrow.

Gracie sat, once again, at the kitchen table, looking out her window, drinking Darjeeling tea from a beautiful china cup. This was the day the Lord had made, and she was rejoicing in it. New fresh snow, as far as she could see, covered the farm, and the red and white curtains still framed the meadows and the barn. Her heart was full of the faithfulness of God. She couldn't help but softly sing:

Great is Thy faithfulness!

Great is Thy faithfulness!

Morning by morning new mercies I see;

all I have needed Thy hand hath provided:

great is Thy faithfulness, Lord, unto me!

"Thank You, precious Jesus!" Gracie prayed while Callie Ann rubbed against her ankles.

"Thank You for saving my little boy and for bringing my mother home." Her Bible lay open to the 23rd Psalm.

"Are you having your morning devotions, Mrs. LeMaster?" Pastor Al interrupted gently as he entered the kitchen.

"Yes, I guess you could say that," she answered. "Would you like some tea or coffee?"

"Yes, coffee, please. It smells so very good. How did you manage with no electricity?"

Gracie took down one of Grammy's best mugs and poured the young man a cup of coffee.

"Cream and sugar's in front of you," she directed him as he sat down at the table with her, and she poured from an old coffee pot she'd filled with coffee grounds and water. "This old wood stove comes in handy if you don't mind 'camp' coffee."

"I don't mind at all."

"Pastor," Gracie began, "why did you come here?"

"I was hoping to get some alone time with you this

Apple Muffin Cottage

morning so we could talk."

"I thought so," Gracie said.

"Mrs. LeMaster," he started.

"Please call me Gracie," she interrupted.

"Let me first say that I'm so happy for you and your family that your mother has returned and for the rescue of your son. Both are miracles, I'm convinced."

"Thank you. I agree. Praise the good Lord for both."

"Next, I knew your husband, Ben, and of course, I am a friend to your brother, Michael."

"Really? You knew Ben? And Michael? My brother seems to be full of surprises these days."

"I was a product of Ben's missionary work in Honduras."

"I see," Gracie said as she started to tense up. "I always resented Ben's trips to Honduras. I'm sorry about that now," she told Pastor Al and smiled sweetly. "How did you end up here?"

"It was a favor to your brother Michael, who is my presbyter, and also, it was because of you."

"Me? Why me?"

"Because I made a promise to God that I would help take care of you and your children someday."

"But why?" Gracie asked again with intensity. "And if that's the case, why were you so rude to me?"

"Forgive me for that, Mrs. LeMaster. I just couldn't face you."

"I want to hear your story, pastor."

"Well, my whole family was converted to Christianity during Ben's first trip to Honduras. I was eleven. We helped him build his mission."

"Al. Ben's friend Al. That's who you are!" Gracie said with excitement.

The young man smiled and shook his head yes.

"I'm the reason that your husband died, Mrs. LeMaster." Tears welled up in his eyes as he looked at Gracie.

"Ben died in a plane crash. Why do you think you're responsible?"

"I received my call into the ministry at eighteen. Pastor Ben was very happy and felt obligated to help me get into

Bible College in Florida."

"I remember that now," Gracie said. "He was very excited about it."

"When everything was arranged and it came time for me to leave Honduras, I became very afraid. And, I'm ashamed to say, for a few short days, turned my back on God. I was in rebellion. I got drunk and went into my grandmother's house and wouldn't come out. 'Alejandro,' my mother would call to me, 'please come out and get ready to go to Florida.' But I wouldn't answer her."

"Then what happened?"

"My mother sent my father to the mission to call your husband to come and help me. He got on that plane for me, Mrs. LeMaster. And because of me and my fear and rebellion, he died when that plane crashed in Honduras. And I am so very sorry."

"Oh, Al," Gracie said as she placed her hand on his arm.

"I promised God that I would go to Bible college and come where you were someday and help see to you and your family. Michael called me and said that he needed a temporary pastor for Hope Springs until he could take it over himself in July or August. I jumped at the chance, especially when he mentioned that you had come back from Brotherton to Spirit Creek Farm. But I was even a coward about that, and when I ran into you for the first time, I was too afraid to face you. I was ashamed. Again, I'm sorry."

"Wow," Gracie said, "what guilt you've had to deal with since then."

"Yes, a lot," he said, "but no more than I deserve."

"Al, let me tell you something that I've never told anyone before," Gracie said. "And because of my children, I would appreciate it if you would not tell anyone."

"Of course, I wouldn't. What is it?"

"A few days before Ben left home, I told him that I was going to have another baby. He didn't seem very happy about it and didn't say much. He was a quiet deep thinker. We had been struggling with our marriage. We were unequally yoked. I was a lukewarm Christian with a career of my own that I thought was more important than what he was doing. When we had Elizabeth, I started nagging at him to stay home. He had wanted me to go on the mission field with him, but I didn't see it as my calling.

Certainly, after I had her, I wasn't going with a new baby or giving up my career. So, when I told him about another baby, I asked him again if he would consider staying home and finding a church to pastor. He said he had already decided that it was time to do that, but he wanted to go back to Honduras to tell his parishioners and his staff that he would be resigning and help them find a replacement. I asked him not to go, but he said it was something he had to do. So, I agreed. He made his plane reservations and flew out the next Monday morning. He'd only been gone about half an hour when I got a call from your father at the Honduran Mission wanting to talk to him. I told him that Ben was on his way back and gave him an ETA. So, you see, Al, it had nothing at all to do with you; it was just circumstances."

Al was startled. "My father never told me. He never knew I thought I was to blame. But, are you sure, Mrs. LeMaster?"

Bruised fruit. That's what Grammy would have called him. Pick him up quickly and gently.

"I'm certain. *You* were *never* to blame."

The young, handsome minister straightened his back and took a long, deep breath, then breathed out slowly and calmly as if the weight of the world had just been lifted from his shoulders and light came back into his eyes.

"I don't know what to say."

"Nothing *to* say. Try one of these muffins. And put lots of butter on it," she said, grinning as she watched joy come into his face.

"I think I will—lots," he chuckled.

"And there is something you can do for me."

"Anything."

"Be my friend and my pastor."

"Always!"

"So, Michael is coming back to pastor Hope Springs Church?" Gracie giggled.

"I really wasn't supposed to tell that," Al said, wiping the last tears from his eyes.

"I won't say anything," Gracie promised, "if you'll have two muffins.

"Deal!" The young man grinned. The guilt had gone, and Gracie was glad.

"Wow! This muffin is delicious, Mrs. LeMaster," he exclaimed with butter on his chin.

"Call me Gracie."

How'd I do with the bruised fruit, Grammy?

***

"Excellent muffins, Elizabeth!" Ian bragged on Gracie's daughter.

"Would you like another?" Elizabeth offered.

"No. No. Watching my waistline." Ian sat back in the dining room chair and patted his stomach.

"Mom, what about you?" Gracie asked Maggie.

"No, thank you. I'm stuffed. I haven't had a breakfast that good since I ate Grammy's cooking." Maggie's eyes seemed to wander off to another time.

Gracie had managed to cook some sausage links to go along with their muffins after she and Al had their talk in the kitchen and he had scrambled some eggs for the other guests. She enjoyed cooking in Grammy's kitchen on the old wood stove with her new friend while he sang praise songs in Spanish. Apple Muffin Cottage *was* better than a Bed and Breakfast. Like the sign by the back door said:

THE BEST FOOD AROUND

"Al, another?" Gracie asked her new friend.

"I'm just going to have some more of your wonderful coffee." He brought back the coffee pot and heated Ian's cup. Maggie and Gracie were having tea.

"Dr. Mac, is Dinky well enough to eat anything yet?" Elizabeth asked about her brother.

"Sure. Just give him what he'll eat. His fever broke around four this morning, and I think he'll sleep for a while, though. He might not be too hungry yet. What he needs most now is plenty of rest and lots to drink when he wakes up."

"I'll make sure he gets it," Elizabeth assured the doctor.

"Are you going to eat anything else, Bethie?" Maggie asked her granddaughter.

"Maybe later, thank you," Elizabeth grinned slightly and answered this strange but beautiful older woman who'd just popped into their lives out of nowhere. It was incredible, almost surreal. This was the "looker" who had ridden out of town with the old hippie in the Corvette all those years ago and left her four children. How was she supposed to feel about her, and how was she supposed to act? Elizabeth was confused, but somehow, she felt a connection to her and knew that there must have been a reason why she left. She liked her and was glad to have a grandmother now.

Maggie smiled at Elizabeth as she headed back into the living room to sit by her little brother.

"She's a beauty, Gracie," Maggie said.

"She looks like you." Gracie smiled at her mother.

"Maggie, I want to tell you something. Ian and Al know our situation. We've talked and decided it's best for now to not expect too much from LaVinia."

"I understand completely."

"Thank you," said Gracie, "but I'm afraid *she* might not, though. You see, I've never mentioned to any of the others that I thought I had found you. I wanted to be sure it *was* you. And it's probably been a pretty big shock to her. And this early in her pregnancy…"

"Oh," Maggie groaned slightly, "do you think it best I go? I don't want to cause problems."

"No! No!" Gracie said loudly. "Please stay. I just want to figure out the best way to handle all of this. It will be okay. If we can just be patient…"

"However you think best," Maggie said, her eyes wide with concern.

"Thank you."

"It's okay," Maggie said softly and almost little-girl-like. She knew this wouldn't be easy, but she was ready to deal with things—good or bad. She'd already received far more understanding than she ever deserved.

"I've met her, Gracie."

"How's that?"

"I've been living at Brotherton Arms for several months. One day last fall, a pretty young woman came in to decorate the mantel and the stairway in the lobby for Christmas. I'd been sitting on the sofa reading a book, and she apologized for interrupting me. I told her it was no problem at all. I enjoyed watching her work. It was absolutely gorgeous when she finished. Red bows, silver bells, pine cones, and greenery. I complimented her. She seemed so familiar to me—her mannerisms, her smile. Then her helper came in and called her by name—LaVinia. Then I knew but thought it best I slip away and say nothing. After New Year's, she came back and took down her decorations. She seemed so pale, and I could tell she was very sick. I had her take a seat until Amy, her helper, got back. I got her a drink of water and felt so helpless. Amy finished taking things down, and they left."

"LaVinia told me about the beautiful lady that was so kind to her there. Of course, she didn't know who you were. Oh, she'll come around. Everything will be alright. She's just stubborn and pregnant. That's not a good combination. That's like the woman with the bumper sticker that said, 'Warning! I'm out of estrogen, and I have a loaded gun.'" Gracie laughed until her sides hurt. *It felt so good to laugh.*

"Oh, my goodness, Gracie girl, you're so funny," Maggie giggled, "I'm so glad I came home."

"Mama, please never leave us again."

"I want to stay, Gracie," Maggie confessed, "if they'll all have me and forgive me."

"They will—in time," Gracie reassured her mother.

***

When Dinky woke up, he found striped Callie Ann beside him on the couch.

"Callie Ann, I sure was cold outside. Would you

believe I saw Pop? He gave me back this old black hat after it blowed away. I couldn't find it, but Pop did."

"What do you mean you saw Pop?" Gracie heard him talking to Callie Ann and was astonished at what she heard. "You were dreaming, sweetie. You were too young to even remember him." By this time, Elizabeth and the others sitting around the crackling fire were listening intently, too.

"I've seen his picture. I don't fink I was dreamin'. I was gonna make a snowman, and that hat flew out of my hand when it started to snow and the wind blowed real hard and I went lookin' for it, but I couldn't see a fing. I couldn't make a snowman without Pop's old hat. But I got so cold and tired and sat down by the old fence post to rest a minute. I heard somebody say somefin' and I looked up and there was Pop. He said, 'Boy, you better keep this old hat on your head and don't take it off.' So I said fanks, and he said, 'I see somebody coming to get ya, so leave it on so they can see ya.' Then I fink I did go to sleep until that angel lady found me."

"And I never would have seen you without that black hat," said Maggie. Gracie had her hand up over her mouth to stifle a cry. Tears flooded her eyes and poured over her cheeks. She remembered the day Pop came to see her when Dinky was born. She handed the tiny infant to her grandfather, and he looked down on him with love and concern and said, "Davis, my boy, you're such a dinky little feller. I think I'll call you Dinky."

As he held his great-grandson in one arm, he reached with the other hand and pulled the baby's little knit cap over his ears and said, "Boy, you'd better keep this hat on your head and keep warm."

Then he looked up at Gracie and said with a sweet smile, "Now, I know you're concerned about this little feller not having his daddy around, but I *promise* ya I'll always help you take care of him."

"Wow, Dinky, I think the Lord allowed Pop to be one of your angels today."

"But he didn't *even* have any wings or a helmet, though. Just an old green coat and a hat."

Ian stepped nervously to the window and looked out through the blue and white curtains onto the porch.

Gracie knew that Dinky had heard her tell stories about Pop a hundred times or more, but she knew also that whatever circumstances saved him, the good Lord had orchestrated them.

"Thank you, dear God!" Gracie whispered.

Promises Kept

The day passed slowly in Apple Muffin Cottage without electricity. Dinky had a nap. Then Elizabeth brought him a plate of her brownies and a cold glass of milk in the late afternoon. Pastor Al and Ian sat at the dining room table, drinking coffee and discussing the Bible. Gracie and Maggie were in the kitchen sitting at Grammy's table, "catching up" while the vegetable beef soup and cornbread were being reheated on the wood stove. While looking out at the rolling fields so white and pristine, Maggie's heart was thrilled just to be back in Grammy's kitchen—again.

She'd loved her mother-in-law and father-in-law dearly, along with this house, her husband Joshua, and their children. They'd had such high hopes for their lives, but life took an unexpected turn—a detour for her of more than thirty years, but she was home now, and there was peace and joy here at Apple Muffin Cottage along with her Gracie, who was faithful, gentle, loving, kind and good.

***

Thud!

"What was that?" Dinky said with his mouth full of a last bite of chocolate brownie. He hopped up on his knees on Grammy's old couch and looked out the window into the yard just in time to see Elizabeth throw another snowball.

Thud!

She smiled and waved to her little brother, who was grinning from ear to ear with chocolate-covered teeth and red cheeks. His hair was in a mass of strawberry-blonde curls. He was feeling much better and giggled as he watched his sister roll up a huge snowball on the ground. Every now and then, his warm breath fogged up the cold window pane, and he would wipe it clear again.

Dinky clapped his hands with joy when Elizabeth held up Pop's old black hat and the bag of snowman fixins that contained two pieces of coal for eyes, Pop's old glasses, a pair of red wax lips, and an old corn cob pipe. And right there, in front of Apple Muffin Cottage's living room window in two feet of snow with a big bright orange carrot in her coat pocket, Elizabeth kept a very important promise: *she* taught Dinky how to make a snowman.

All the while, she heard another faint promise of forever on the wind through the orchards—a violin softly playing:

Yes, we'll gather at the river,

Promises Kept

The beautiful, the beautiful river;

Gather with the saints at the river

That flows by the throne of God…

Grammy's and Gracie's Favorite Recipes and Crafts

Recipe: *Grace Barton's Blue Ribbon Apple Muffins*

It's a secret (only Bethie knows!).

Recipe: Grammy's Turkey Stuffing

Make two pans of cornbread. Let it cool. Tear up cornbread into a big bowl. Salt a bit, but be careful. Add a little sugar if you want, but not needed. Cook turkey giblets and turkey neck in chicken broth til done. Strain broth. Add 3 to 4 chopped onions, 5 or 6 stalks (chopped) of celery, plus celery leaves and sage or poultry seasoning (to taste—not too much) to broth and cook til tender. Once done, add two sticks of butter and let them melt. Pour over cornbread. Let it soak in. Cut up giblets and take the meat off turkey neck if you want and add to stuffing. If not, put in freezer until you can use them for something. If not moist enough, add more broth.

Recipe: Diamonds-In-the-Snow Cupcakes

(for little Gracie): Use a white moist cake mix, use only egg whites in it instead of whole eggs, and bake cupcakes in white or light blue papers.

Let cool and frost with a cream cheese frosting.

Sprinkle with sanding sugar for twinkle effect.

Apple Muffin Cottage

Recipe: *Grammy's Valentine's Day Fudge Brownies:*

I quadruple the fudge brownie recipe in the Better Homes and Gardens Cookbook.

I make a big batch so you can cut them out easier with heart cookie cutters. Stack two or three heart brownies on top of each other, once cooled, and wrap in plastic wrap, gather at top, and tie up with a red ribbon (when giving away) or put on a plate and serve with cherry pie filling and whipped cream.

Notes: _Grapefruit Bird Feeder_

1. Clean out the inside of half a grapefruit rind.
2. Poke three holes around the top of it about ½ inch down (equally spaced).
3. Cut three 18-inch lengths of red ribbon and tie a knot at one end of each.
4. Pull the unknotted end of each ribbon through one of the holes from the inside out.
5. Tie the three unknotted ends of the ribbons together at the top.
6. Mix ½ cup of birdseed with ¼ cup of peanut butter and fill grapefruit rind.
7. Hang anywhere outside for birds.

Apple Muffin Cottage

Notes: *Snowman Fixins*

1 corncob (or any kind) pipe, 1 pair of red wax lips with hole for pipe to go through, 2 pieces of coal, pair of old glasses—put in drawstring bag and set in old hat of some kind.

Add a bright orange carrot from the crisper drawer the day snowman is built.

Put a scarf on him if you want to.

Recipe: Snow Day Hot Chocolate

Use the recipe off of the side of Hershey's Cocoa Box. Serve warm with little marshmallows.

Recipe: **Gracie's Meatballs:**

Add 1 cup of chili sauce or BBQ sauce to one cup of peach or apricot jam per 25 frozen meatballs in a slow cooker. Cook until meatballs are hot through and sauce is a little cooked down.

Recipe: Gracie's Veggie Beef Soup

Brown 2 lbs of ground beef or ground turkey, drain and add to 2 boxes of chicken broth, 2 chopped onions, ½ small head of chopped cabbage, two cans of mixed veggies or any kind of veggies, one jar of marinara sauce, ¼ cup ketchup, 1 tablespoon of marjoram, 1 tablespoon of thyme. Add a handful of elbow macaroni for a heartier soup if you like.

Cook just to boiling, reduce heat, cover, and simmer for 45 minutes.

Good served with shredded cheese and cornbread.

Apple Muffin Cottage

Recipe: Gracie LeMaster's Chicken Soup:

Chop up 1 large onion, 4-5 stalks of celery, and add to 2 or 3 boxes of chicken broth.

Cook until tender. Add 3 boneless chicken breasts, cooked and cubed. Add 4-5 medium-sized potatoes, peeled and cubed, and cook until just tender. Add a stick of butter. Salt carefully. Add a cup of cream if desired.

If for a cold, add 3-4 smashed cloves of garlic and leave out cream and butter.

Keep watching for more as *The Farmwell Valley Series* continues…

Holleyhock Haven

Patchwork Parsonage

Melody Manor

Apple Muffin Cottage